Stevie's Secret

Stevie's Secret

A novel by
Diane Shader Smith

This book is for my husband Mark, and our two children, Micah and Mallory.

Copyright 1999© Diane Shader Smith
All rights reserved.
Printed in the United States of America

ISBN 0-9700353-1-4

Rev. 09/00

Chapter 1

Stevie Jaeger stood on the tips of her toes trying to get a peek at the bulletin board in the gym. She was 14 years old, but at only 5'1" and 80 pounds, she felt dwarfed by the other high school students around her. Dozens of kids had gathered to read the instructions for dance company auditions. Stevie wished she could see more than the backs of their heads.

Now that Stevie was a freshman at Riverdale High School, she had two goals: to get into the dance company and to start dating. Stevie had never had a boyfriend. She'd had plenty of crushes, but none had materialized into a relationship. There was a really cute guy in her algebra class, and another in homeroom. But neither of those boys compared to the one leaning against the wall on the side of the gym. He had a girl on each arm, and was flirting wildly with both of them.

Stevie's stomach flip-flopped. She wondered if there really was such a thing as love at first sight. If so, then this was it. His thick, shoulder-length hair was loosely tied back in a ponytail. When he turned to greet some other friends, Stevie saw that his lips were also thick, and turned down just a bit at the corner of his mouth, giving him a mischievous look. He might also be the only guy in high school who could success-fully grow facial hair.

Close to six feet tall, he had a swimmer's body — broad shoulders and narrow hips. He looked like a jock, but unlike most high school athletes, who loped along, loose-limbed, this guy seemed really comfortable with his body. As he walked, Stevie saw that he moved with a dancer's poise. He was light on his feet, but more than that, it was the way his muscles moved; he seemed to be in complete control of them. His hair was brown with reddish high-lights, and his skin was olive. Stevie straightened herself. She would have liked to watch him more, but he was off before she had the chance.

"Do you know who that is?" Stevie asked a girl from her homeroom, trying to sound as casual as possible.

"Kyle Matthews," Victoria replied. "He's incredible!"

"Girlfriend?" Stevie couldn't help herself.

"Irrelevant," Victoria shot back. "He's a junior."

Katie, another freshman, raised her eyebrows. "I heard some girl named Maddie Phillips snagged him over the summer."

"Unverified," Victoria said.

"How does everyone know him?" Stevie was curious.

"He danced a solo last year," Victoria answered. "Didn't you see him in concert? I thought you were the big dance aficionado."

"I missed the concert last year," Stevie said, examining her cuticle. She didn't want to say what had kept her away.

Victoria looked puzzled. Katie asked if either of them wanted to go for a soda.

"No, thanks," Stevie said. "I'm waiting to get a look at the bulletin board." She didn't want to sound uninterested, but there was no way she would admit to her new friends what she had to do after school.

Stevie had a secret ... one only a handful of people knew. She had cystic fibrosis, a serious genetic disease. She didn't tell people because she didn't want to be pitied. She didn't want to be different. Being a teenager was tough, but being a teenager with cystic fibrosis was unbearable. Labeled "failure to thrive" shortly after birth, she'd always had trouble maintaining her weight, and consistently measured below the fifth percentile for her age group.

There were plenty of other disadvantages to

CF, such as chronic lung infections and bowel obstructions. Also, she had to do treatments each day to clear the sticky mucus from her lungs, and she had to take a lot of pills. Every morning, she took Adeks, a prescription pill containing the four fat-soluble vitamins, and every time she ate she took Ultrase digestive enzyme supplements. But the most embarrassing aspect for Stevie was delayed onset of puberty; she was the only one of her friends who hadn't gotten her period. Worse, she was completely flat-chested.

Stevie had learned early on to rely on clothes to make her look bigger. Fashion and teen magazines had great suggestions, but the clothes they advertised were always so pricey. And money was definitely an issue. It had been ever since her dad had died and her mom had gone back to work.

Stevie didn't have any siblings, but Lucy Chaplin, who lived next door, had served as a surrogate big sis before leaving for college. It was Lucy who had introduced Stevie to the idea of shopping at vintage clothing stores. For the past few years, Stevie and her best friend Clara Daniels had spent the first Saturday of each month stretching their allowances at Paradise Thrift Shop, selecting the best of the $5 bellbottoms and $10 cashmere sweaters. In building her wardrobe, she had followed the top five bests for short girls — monochromatic outfits, patterns with small prints, short skirts, pleated pants, and pedal pushers. Platforms were a no-brainer.

Stevie looked around to see who else was trying out. As she noticed what some of the other girls were wearing, she felt a slow flush creep across her face. Maybe the outfit she had chosen for her first day of high school was too bright; she had on a yellow bumblebee-patterned dress and navy boots with thick-soled bottoms. She really felt like a freshman.

The only time Stevie didn't feel small was when she was dancing. Dancing, Stevie was able to soar; as she lost herself in movement, she found herself. Her true self. The self that had nothing to do with CF.

Gradually, Stevie was able to inch her way towards the front. Auditions were in the gym the following afternoon. Those interested were to report to Studio A in black leotards and tights, ready to dance at 3:21. The final school bell rang at 3:14, so there wouldn't be much time to change and get to the gym.

Some of the girls in Stevie's homeroom had talked briefly about trying out, but she didn't know if they were serious about dancing. Clara was planning to audition, but she hadn't taken more than a few classes in her life. Mia Detaille, the artistic director, was not known to accept freshmen, and Clara didn't hold out much hope. Even Stevie, who had been taking dance classes since she was five, knew her chances were slim.

But her heart told her she had worked too hard not to try. Freshmen had been accepted occasionally in the past. It wasn't impossible.

Stevie walked into the bank where her mom worked. She went to the staff lounge and tossed her backpack on the table. Seeing Alex Callahan brought a smile to her face. He was in on it. He could be trusted. Alex was a part-time teller, who at the moment was comfortably ensconced on an old gray sofa, reading the comics. He often sat with Stevie to keep her company during her CF treatments.

Stevie's mother opened a vial of Albuterol solution and poured it into a nebulizer cup. Then she fitted a face mask over the cup and connected it to an air pump with a rubber hose. She slipped the mask strap around Stevie's head, and turned the pump on. A fine mist swirled through the mask around Stevie's face. Stevie had to wear the mask and inhale the mist for 15 minutes to open up the passageways in her lungs.

When that was finished, she sat on her mom's lap while her mom did chest percussion therapy on her, pounding Stevie's back and chest in eight positions for three minutes each using little blue paddles. The entire routine took about 45 minutes. She did this three times a day: before school, after school, and before bedtime. Stevie hated treatment because it was way too time-consuming. Also, it was humiliating to sit in her mom's lap. She couldn't imagine her friends doing any such thing.

"Can we cut a few minutes today?" Stevie asked.

"You know I hate to do that," her mom replied.

"But my PFTs were way up last month and I've got stuff to do," said Stevie. PFTs were the results of the pulmonary function test Stevie took each quarter to measure how much air was getting into her lungs. Good results meant her lungs weren't filled with mucus and could function almost normally.

"Don't whine," her mom said absently. Then she looked up. "Do you have homework already, sweetie?"

"Dance company tryouts. Tomorrow, right after school. I'll have to skip my afternoon treatment. All week if I make the callbacks."

"And if you get in?"

Stevie flushed, realizing she hadn't thought this part through. Afternoon treatments had been part of her CF protocol since her hospitalization last year. It hadn't been a problem until now, since her daily routine consisted of school, treatment, snack and then dance class.

Now her mom was quiet but firm. "I'm sorry, Stevie. I have to say no. You can't participate in dance company if it means missing your afternoon treatment. It's just not worth it."

Stevie went ballistic. "How can you tell me

7

it's not worth it? How do you know? I'm the one who's worked my whole life for this!"

"I know how important dancing is to you, and there's no reason for you to stop. But you don't need to be in a company. You can keep taking classes at Eastside Ballet …"

"Forget it, Mom!" Stevie was adamant. "I am auditioning for dance company tomorrow, and you can't stop me."

"Stevie!" Her mom's voice rang out as Stevie slammed the door of the staff lounge behind her. She ran through the bank and outside into the cold air, feeling bad about abandoning both her treatment and her mother.

Chapter 2

There were two minutes until the audition rehearsal was scheduled to begin, and Stevie had ducked into the locker room to change. She had already slipped out of her skirt and shirt, and had pulled on her tights and leotard, only dimly aware of the other girls nervously chatting around her. She glanced at her watch, then ran to the sink with her makeup pouch.

Before school each day, Stevie rushed through treatment and breakfast; there wasn't time for makeup. Being glam wasn't super-important to her, but she always wanted to look older. Today, she wanted to look like a serious dancer, so makeup was a must.

Working quickly, she pulled out her bottle of Sand base and tipped it gently onto her sponge. Then she dotted and wiped the liquid over her cheeks, nose and forehead. With a Q-tip, she smudged White Shimmer below her brow and worked a pop of Midnight Blue into the crease of her eyelid. With a brush she'd bought at Macy's last Christmas, she swept Bronze Goddess across her cheeks, working it upwards as the lady at the counter had shown her. Finally, she opened a tube of Plum lip gloss and dabbed at her lips. She pulled her blonde hair away from her face and pinned it, ballerina style, at the nape of her neck. Stevie smiled. She was ready.

Stevie ran back into the dance studio as Mia Detaille was giving instructions to what looked like 150 students. Auditions were held in a large room with mirrors on three of the four walls. A long, wooden *barre* ran along both of the side walls. The studio was similar to the one at Eastside Ballet, but at Eastside, there had never been more than 30 dancers at any given time.

Mia's voice was strong and clear through the microphone. "We'll learn one routine — a ballet, modern and jazz combination that we'll rehearse today and tomorrow. Not to worry if you haven't studied ballet; we don't go *en pointe*. I just need to see if you can catch on. No judging yet, but Thursday you're up. Friday will be callbacks. If you make it, you'll perform the combination and also a minute and a half of your own choreography. Your own work should feature your best stuff. If you're a tapper, show me some tap. If you do an amazing split jump, I want to see it. Company will be posted on Monday. There shouldn't be any questions, so I'm not taking any."

Mia's reputation was legendary. She was in her mid 40s but looked much younger. Her chestnut brown hair was always piled on top of her head, and she wore funky cat's eye tortoise-shell glasses. Her tone was tough, and she expected 100% commitment. She was a harsh taskmaster, but the dancers respected her because she really delivered at concert time.

Even more intimidating were the members of Company, who were cliquey and judged their peers on the basis of grade level, talent and charisma. Stevie sighed. She knew she had set her sights high, but this was the way to begin.

All the auditioners stood up and spaced themselves around the studio. Stevie scanned the sea of faces until she saw Kyle. Her heart pounded. She watched as he moved to the front of the studio. Stevie wanted to follow, but changed her mind as she saw Terra Reede leap towards him. The most sensational dancer in Company, Terra had sleek brown hair and a shapely body. Kyle put his arms out to catch her, and they spun around until they collapsed on the floor, laughing.

"You're my dance darling," Terra declared theatrically, pulling him up.

"And you're my pretty princess," Kyle said, dipping her dramatically.

Stevie's heart sank. Were they an item?

Mia clapped her hands, calling the group to

order, and turned on a Dave Matthews CD. Moving to its lyrical melody, she demonstrated an *adagio*. The choreography featured a slow center-floor sequence. As Mia danced, she called out the movements: "*Developé* 2, 3, 4 and rotate 2, 3, 4. *Ponché* 2, 3, 4, and torso up, leg down through to fourth."

After most of the dancers had mastered the steps, Mia changed the music to a Janet Jackson remix and led them through a jazz routine: "Walk-walk-kick-ball-change. Pose 1, pose 2, pose 3, pose 4. Swivel-swivel-outside turn and open-second."

The rhythmic beat of African drums came next, and the choreography was spare. "This is modern, people," Mia commanded. "Contract in second position, leg swings behind, pivot. Extend your arm and reach and reach and fall. Slowly rise and reach and reach and fall. Now take it once again from the top."

"You're lucky you've had so many lessons," Clara whispered as she struggled to keep up. Stevie ached for Clara. Her friend was wavering, missing beats, then shuffling to catch up. Looking around, Stevie was amazed at the range of talent in one room. She felt sorry for the ones who had no chance of making it.

"Hang in there," she said to Clara, hoping to infuse as much warmth as possible into her words.

Two hours into pre-auditions, Mia called a

break. Stevie and Clara were panting as they stepped to the side. The vigor of the dancing made Stevie start coughing, and she couldn't stop. A cluster of dancers were leaning against the *barre*, stretching and flexing as they relaxed. They turned to stare at Stevie. Clara put a reassuring hand on Stevie's shoulder and whispered to her. "Just say you've got a tickle in your throat."

Stevie smiled, but Clara's words didn't help. She felt mad at herself for making so much noise. Once again, having CF was a major embarrassment. Terra strutted by, and shot Stevie a look of irritation.

Finally, the spasm stopped. Stevie worked up her nerve and walked over to Terra. "Excuse me," she said tentatively.

"What?" Terra snapped back, without looking at her.

Stevie summoned up her courage. "You're amazing."

Terra sounded annoyed. "Thanks." She left quickly.

Clara edged to her side. "No shortage of attitude on her part."

Grateful that Clara was a good friend, Stevie shrugged. "She knows she's good."

"That's no excuse for being rude," said Clara.

Another girl had seen the exchange and offered her opinion. "She knows the only thing that's standing between her and a career on stage is about 15 pounds."

Stevie was surprised. "She looks fine. She's not overweight."

The girl shook her head. "She thinks she is. Terra's tried every diet in the book. Auditions for Rusty Carmichael's Company are next month."

"Doesn't she want to go to college?" Stevie asked.

"Only part time," the girl said. "Dancing is the only thing that matters to Terra."

"If that's true, she'd better get on it. Time is running out," Clara said.

The reference to time jarred Stevie. She glanced at her watch, knowing that by now her mother had gotten the message Stevie had left for her saying she wouldn't be coming for treatment today. Her mom would be furious. Stevie stiffened, then willed herself not to care. Her mother would come around. Her health had been good lately. Besides, her mom made too big a deal about everything to do with CF.

Stevie was hoping to get home before her mother. She wanted to be in her bedroom when her mom confronted her. Their fights went better when Stevie was able to set the stage: she was sure to be less angry if she found Stevie sitting at her desk doing homework than if Stevie was watching TV or talking on the phone.

Since the garage door was closed, Stevie didn't know if she had beaten her mother home or not. She used her key to open the front door, and felt her heart sink; the aroma of rosemary chicken told her that her mom was already there. Stevie threw her backpack on the entry hall table just as her mother came out of the kitchen.

"You went to the audition." Her mother's voice was tinged with anger.

Stevie flattened herself against the wall in the entrance hall. "I had to," she said, and waited.

When her mother spoke again, her voice was higher pitched and strained. "I'm worried about you."

"It's my problem," Stevie responded.

Her mother crossed over to her. The heels of her pumps clattered across the wood. This time, she spoke quietly and gently. "It's both of ours, Stevie. We've always worked together as a team. That's why you've done so well until now. If you start skipping your afternoon treatment, I don't know what will happen." Her mom sank down until she was sitting on the bottom step of the staircase. Her legs were tucked under her, and she looked young, almost girlish.

"Mom. It'll be okay."

Her mom looked at her wordlessly for a moment. Then she drew herself up. "Your ballet academy is much better than any high school dance company could be. You were having a great dance experience and I'm afraid this will move you away from classical training."

"I've done ballet. Now I want to do modern, jazz and hip-hop," Stevie said. "Besides, I'll be getting more exercise. Hip-hop and jazz take a lot of energy."

Stevie's mom shook her head. "Exercise is no substitute for treatment. Dr. Bowman says doing a treatment mid-day is critical."

Stevie's exasperation was palpable. "I didn't do it before my hospitalization last year! I don't want to do it now!"

Her mother slammed her hand against the wall, then stood up. Her voice was sharp, but she was clearly trying to control her anger. "You don't think what I have to say is important. Maybe you'll believe me when you hear the same thing from Dr. Bowman. You have your appointment on Thursday and we'll talk to him then."

Stevie felt herself going slack. Clinic appointments were always the same: the waiting room was crowded, her mom was tense. Stevie carried her portable CD player and focused on the lyrics of The Beastie Boys or Alanis Morrisette. She tried not to notice the other patients, who were skinny, hacking away, and clearly wishing that they, too, were somewhere else.

"Dr. Bowman is going to side with you," Stevie blurted. "He always does."

"Stevie," her mother said, stroking her hair the way she'd done since Stevie was little. "You wanted to skip treatment the day of your eighth grade prom so you could get your hair done with your girlfriends, remember? I didn't think it was a good idea, but Dr. Bowman said, 'You only have one eighth grade prom.'"

Stevie stared at her mother. "Dance company is every day. He'll say no."

"He's reasonable," her mother argued. "He'll come up with a compromise."

"Postpone the appointment until next Thursday. I won't know until then if I'm even in Company," Stevie pleaded with her mom.

Her mom smiled. "Ever hear of the word 'please?'"

Chapter 3

Stevie walked into the studio after school on Wednesday and immediately saw Mia's posted note that she'd be late. Stevie sighed and stretched, using her bends as an excuse to look over at Kyle, who stood to her left. He was helping Terra, who lay on her back with her leg up in the air. Kyle held her ankle, and with each count of ten pushed her leg a little closer to stretch out her hamstring. Kyle smiled at Stevie, but Stevie instantly averted her eyes. She was busted for staring and way too embarrassed to smile back.

Mia came in and called the group to order.

"Listen up. I'm going to demonstrate a hip-hop routine." It was kind of funky, the steps rapid and jerky. She kept most of her body weight very low to the ground. "Keep it sly," Mia directed. "Give me rhythm with a sassy attitude."

Stevie had watched a lot of MTV; now she thought of the blank-faced girls who danced to the lyrics, and made her body supple and loose. Around her, the footwork was in sync. But every so often, someone would miss a step and throw off the line of motion. Mia pointedly ignored the dancers who were having trouble. Stevie couldn't help but mentally dismiss them as well, but narrowing the field made her acutely aware of the competition. She was up against some really good dancers. Stevie took a breath as she turned, leaned and thrust her hip out.

After dinner, Stevie thought about what had happened during the first round of auditions. It was a big blur. She guessed that only about 75 students had actually shown up. They had filed in with signed audition forms, and had been assigned to groups of four. Each group had performed all of the material they'd been taught that week. After they had finished, they were dismissed.

Stevie went to bed that night, unsure of how she'd done. She didn't really know how to evaluate herself. She wasn't sure what Mia was looking for.

The next morning, the names of dancers who had made the callbacks were on a list posted outside the gym. Just as Stevie walked in, she bumped into Clara, who wasn't smiling. "Bad news?" Stevie asked.

"Not for you. They took 21 and you're one of

them. Not that I'm surprised. You deserve it. You should be happy," Clara said. She was trying to smile, but Stevie saw the tears in her eyes.

"I'm really sorry you didn't make it," Stevie said, giving her a hug. The bell rang. Stevie and Clara headed to their homerooms.

After school, Stevie ran back to the gym. Mia had posted the assignments. This time they were grouped by three. Martha, Sally and Neil were asked to stay and the rest were sent into the hallway. Stevie pulled out an emery board and filed her nails to pass the time and to dissipate her anxiety while she waited.

Twenty minutes later, she was called in with two other girls. Each of them did a minute and a half of her own choreography. Stevie did a ballet routine set to the song, "I Want You Back," by 'N Sync. In the first few seconds she panicked, and lost her concentration. But then she used the beat of the music to steady herself, and quickly recovered her focus. She felt she gave an energized performance — she always felt good about her ballet.

After every person had danced, Mia called them all back in. "I'm going to send some of you home, and keep others a little longer."

"If you send us home now, are we out?" asked a girl with a New York accent.

Mia spoke sternly. "It's important that you not second-guess what I'm doing. Finding just the right dancers for Company is complicated. Sometimes I see immediately what I need. Sometimes I need to keep you longer. Eileen, Josh, April and Sara can go. The rest of you will dance again. Thank you very much. Results will be posted on Monday."

Stevie was sent into the hallway while three of the remaining dancers performed again. This time it only took a few minutes before Stevie was called in. She was grouped with a girl named Nellie and another named Liza. "Stevie, please dance the modern phrase for me," Mia said.

Stevie did as she was told. Nellie went second and Liza third. Mia waited until the three of them were finished before sending Stevie, by herself, into the hallway. She was absolutely convinced she would be axed, because modern was not her forte.

Another ten minutes went by and Stevie was asked to come in and do individual ballet *jetés* across the floor. She felt her legs form a straight horizontal line underneath each jump and experienced a rush of adrenaline. Her years of ballet had paid off.

"That will be all, Stevie," Mia said.

Stevie was crushed. She knew Mia had said not to worry about the time you were sent home but the tone of voice Mia had used made Stevie feel it was over for her.

Chapter 4

Stevie did her best to keep busy all weekend. First she experimented with two new hairstyles. One was super curly, a look she achieved with a quick dry and a half-inch curling iron. Stevie then flipped her head over and shook the curls out. The look was dramatic but too nighttime for school.

The other was a beehive, a style her mother hated the minute she saw it. Stevie separated her hair into sections, teased each part to the ends, flattened it and then repeated the process until all her hair was built into a beehive. Using heavy hairspray, she plastered her head to hold all her hair in place. It was hideous but hilarious.

When she was all dressed up with nowhere to go, she invited Clara to go roller-blading. While they were blading, the wind whipped through her hair, messing it all up. Afterwards, she and Clara drank orange juice in the kitchen. Then Clara had to go. So Stevie cleaned her closet, completed a science project that wasn't due for another few weeks, sent e-mails to her friend Cindy and her favorite aunt, Meryl, and read about the origins of hip-hop.

Stevie vacillated between hope and fatalistic dread. She repeatedly reminded herself that only a handful of freshmen had ever gotten into Company. If it didn't happen this year, she would still have three more years to try. That thought didn't cheer her up, but it kept her from sinking deeper into despair as she recounted all the steps she might have done better.

Stevie knew the bravest souls would show up before school on Monday to find out who'd made it. She was afraid she'd have to suffer through the day with red-rimmed eyes if the news was bad. She had determined to wait until after school, but changed her mind late Sunday night. She set her alarm for 5:30, and jumped out of bed on Monday morning to get an early start on treatment.

Stevie went straight to the gym before school started, but she wasn't the first to arrive. She waited for a mob of girls to move aside, then scanned the alphabetized list several times, looking for her own name. After checking the J's three times, she realized she wasn't on the list. Stevie could feel her eyes burning. How foolish she'd been to pack a bag for rehearsal. She put her index fingers on her temples and squeezed hard, hoping to prevent the tears from flowing.

"Congratulations, Stevie Jaeger." An unfamiliar voice came out of nowhere.

Stevie jumped and turned around but stopped short when she found herself face to face with Kyle. Her cheeks blazing with embarrassment, she stammered, "But I didn't get in."

"Of course you did," Kyle sounded sure of himself.

Beads of perspiration were collecting above her brow. She was confused. She'd read the list. Was he teasing her? If so, he was incredibly cruel. But a question ran through her mind: how did he know her name?

"You're the only freshman to make apprentice," he said. "See for yourself if you don't believe me." Kyle pulled the list off the bulletin board and handed it to her.

"It's not there." Stevie tucked her head down. Kyle turned the sheet over and pointed to the word "Apprentice." Directly underneath it read "Stevie Jaeger." Hers was the only name on the page.

Stevie was speechless.

"Surprised?" he ventured. "Mia rarely takes an apprentice, but when she does, the person is always listed on the back. Sort of establishes the pecking order."

Before Stevie could answer, Terra sidled up

to Kyle and threw her arms around his neck. "Hello," she purred.

"Hi Terra," he replied. "Have you met our new apprentice, Stevie Jaeger? I was just about to introduce myself. I'm Kyle Matthews."

Unsure what to do, Stevie stuck her hand out. Kyle picked her up and gave her a bear hug. "You're a part of Company now," he declared. "That makes us family."

Terra stared down her nose. "Congratulations, apprentice."

Stevie heard the acid in her tone. She knew she was being put in her place; an apprentice wasn't really in Company. The first bell rang, saving Stevie from thinking up a response.

"I'm outta here. Show up at 3:20 and I'll introduce you around," Kyle said, rushing off.

Terra lingered a minute longer. Stevie felt Terra's eyes on her and squirmed inwardly. She knew she looked short and bony. Stevie opened her mouth to speak, but Terra hoisted her backpack over her shoulder.

"Later," she said flipping her hair.

Stevie, stung by Terra's dismissal, decided to focus instead on Kyle. "Show up at 3:20 and I'll introduce you around," he had said. She replayed the scene in her mind. "I'll introduce you around." "Show up at 3:20." Oh no, she thought. What about treatment? How could she tell her mother that she had actually gotten into Company and wouldn't be able to do an after-school treatment?

Chapter 5

At 3:20, Stevie changed into her black leotard and tights, and then went to the studio. She couldn't avoid the feeling that she should be home doing treatment, but she was not about to miss her first day of Company.

Kyle and three other guys were standing near the corner laughing. She saw that most of the boys were wearing bright cotton pants, sweats or boxers. A group of girls were warming up with leg stretches and flexing, dressed in doctor's scrubs and T-shirts, or boxers and cotton dance pants. Terra was alone, in baggy linen pants and a loose-fitting T-shirt, leaning against the *barre*.

Stevie was embarrassed to be the only one in a leotard and tights. She didn't know that black was the uniform for auditions only. As Stevie moved to find a place to stretch, she overheard fragments of conversations about dieting, movies and homework. She sat close to Terra, but not so close as to look like a groupie.

After Kyle finished changing, he flopped down next to Stevie and grabbed her hand. "Have you heard that Company is one big dysfunctional family?"

His eyes were bright, his teeth white against his dark complexion. Stevie hoped Kyle wouldn't notice her nervousness. She shook her head so her voice wouldn't quaver. She couldn't believe he was not only sitting next to her, he was holding her hand.

"Put 30 prima donnas all together in one room, it's gonna be crazy," Kyle continued with a grin. "Let me point out who the major players are. You know Mia. She's not the dance director, she's the dance dictator."

Kyle pointed out a pretty girl with glasses who sat on the piano bench, her fingers flitting over the keys. Too bad the high notes she played were so jarringly out of tune, Stevie thought. "Nellie's boy-crazy," Kyle said.

"That description applies to every girl in here," remarked a blonde girl who had come over to bat her lashes at Kyle. Stevie recognized her but didn't know her name. "Stevie, meet Heather, resident flirt."

"Nice to meet you," Stevie smiled weakly.

Heather smiled at Kyle. "Can you drive me to the Tea Leaf after school?"

27

"Sure," Kyle said, grinning.

Stevie couldn't bear to think that he was interested in Heather. To distract herself from that thought, she looked around the room, studying the scene. Two dancers lay sprawled in the corner.

"Juliana and Laura," Kyle reported. "They're inseparable."

Several dancers sat gossiping in another cranny of the spacious studio. Kyle said Nikki, Jocelyn and Matthew were the ones facing the wall, stretching their calf muscles. Two others were seated with their feet pressed up against each other, talking in murmured tones, and using exaggerated hand gestures to convey the vivid importance of whatever they were saying.

"Jeremy's on the left," Kyle said. "He's quiet. Josh is full of himself but always fun."

Jocelyn walked over to Kyle. "Can you stretch me?"

Kyle nodded and turned to Stevie. "We'll finish this later."

Stevie wished Kyle was working out with her but she knew it would be a long time before she would ask him for a favor. She turned to watch the others. A guy and a girl were crouched by the stereo, humming along with a New Age ballad. A large group was gathered around the portable tape player, which blasted out a rap song. They were shouting over the noise, grooving to the beat of the drums.

Two girls pored over a calculus textbook and

struggled with the formulas. One threw her book down in disgust. She picked up a fashion magazine and approached it with equal gravity.

The one Kyle had identified as Nellie was now sprinting after Josh, who had snatched her Cheetos. When she caught up to him, she jumped on his back and wrestled him to the ground. He wriggled away from her, grabbed the snack bag and took off again. Stevie bit her lip to keep from smiling.

Mia moved to the front of the room, holding an oversized clipboard. "Congratulations to all of you," she said with a smile. It changed the whole look of her face. "In 12 weeks, we will present our concert to the student body. Between now and then, I will transform you from wannabe dancers to professional-caliber performers." Mia's face returned to her usual expression of crisp authority.

"If you've been in Company before, you can audition a piece you've choreographed for concert. I'll post a sign-up sheet in the hallway. Some of you will choose to tell a story, others will be more abstract. I'm only looking for seven or eight dances from within Company, so the competition will be fierce."

"And the solo?" Terra asked.

"Anyone can try."

"As if there's any doubt," muttered a girl wearing all white.

"What about a guest piece?" someone asked.

"Two from professional choreographers. One alumni piece. Jackie Schneider will probably do it. I'm still playing phone tag with her."

"Jackie's awesome," Kyle whispered to Stevie.

"I've seen her dance," Stevie was proud to say. She had seen her many times on television, and recently she'd choreographed a dance concert downtown. Stevie had volunteered as an usher so she could see it for free.

Mia plowed on. "We'll do two rounds of auditions with six or seven dances in each. I know exactly what I'm looking for. I have the vision to pull this together. We can't have too many similar dances. In some cases, your music will be changed. Recasting may be required if someone is in two dances that rehearse at the same time."

Looking at her clipboard, Mia continued with her agenda. She covered rehearsal times, attendance, and cleaning weekend. Stevie didn't know what cleaning weekend was, but she didn't want to look ignorant. Fortunately, a guy raised his hand. He looked young and confused. Maybe he was a sophomore who was also new.

"The weekend before concert we come in very early in the morning on Saturday and Sunday and stay well into the night," Mia explained. "You get a ten-minute break mid-morning and mid-afternoon, and 30 minutes for lunch. We clean each dance, which means we polish it to perfection. Every count must be together, every movement the same. I critique one in the auditorium while a student choreographer works on another in the studio. Pieces rotate through until we've done each one twice."

Panic set in. Stevie knew how worried her mother was about her skipping afternoon treatment. She would flip when she heard about the hours required during cleaning weekend.

Mia moved on. "We will hold a garage sale to raise money for concert the first Saturday in November. I want anything that you or your family can part with. Knickknacks, clothes, paintings, pots and pans. Keep in mind that a chipped porcelain statue of a kitten might be a treasure to a cat lover."

"My father doesn't live with us anymore. He left some books that we don't need," said a lanky boy with spiky hair. "Do you want them?"

"Absolutely," Mia said, and looked back at her clipboard. "Next item is secret buddies." She explained that Company had been doing secret buddies for nine years. Each person in Company drew a name out of a hat to pick a secret buddy, then showered that buddy with inexpensive gifts, notes in his or her locker, or a picnic treat. "Be creative," Mia emphasized, "but don't spend a lot of money. Remember, the key to making this fun is the word 'secret.'"

She took out a top hat filled with slips of paper and passed it around. The girl who drew first smirked at her selection. Terra was next, giggling at the whole thing. One boy with glasses rolled his eyes, while another remained stone-faced.

Stevie turned her neck ever so slightly so she could see Kyle's reaction. The corners of his lips turned up, but Stevie couldn't quite call it a smile. He handed her the hat, and she pulled out a slip of paper with Josh's name on it. All Stevie really knew about Josh was that he was a senior and had the reputation of being snide. Kyle had said he was lots of fun. The hat made its way around the room until everyone had had a turn.

"Let's dance," Mia called out.

Kyle jumped up and pulled Stevie to her feet. Terra came over and grabbed Kyle's hand. She lifted his arm and put it around her shoulder. She acts like she owns him, Stevie thought. Mia turned on a CD of No Doubt, and the class followed in a warm-up routine they'd learned during auditions. Terra whispered to Kyle as they went through the steps. "I hate my history teacher."

"Too much homework?"

"My issue is with the quality, not the quantity. Useless busy work. She's an absolute despot, completely close-minded. Acts like memorizing a bunch of dates will make a difference."

Kyle's voice was a little ragged from exertion, but his tone was firm. "Those who forget the past are condemned to repeat it."

"Not! There are gang wars in the street every

day. People abusing their children. Peace comes only with true awareness, and awareness comes only with self-knowledge."

Moving in time to "Tragic Kingdom," Stevie strained to listen to Terra and Kyle, wondering if she would ever be able to participate in such a mature conversation. She wished she could summon the confidence to join in. She rehearsed in her mind what she would say: "People learn history and repeat it, regardless. They don't apply the lessons to their specific situations."

It sounded so intelligent when she said it to herself. But she was sure that if she tried to say it out loud, it would come out all jumbled and confused.

When rehearsal was over, some of the dancers rushed out, while others dawdled as they collected their things and chatted. Stevie quietly asked Mia if she could have a word with her. Mia motioned her to the far side of the room.

"Thank you for accepting me," Stevie began.

Mia looked at her through her glasses. "You're in because you're good. I don't often take an apprentice."

"Do you know about my medical history?"

"That you have cystic fibrosis? Yes. But I understand that dancing isn't a problem for you. I talked with the nurse after I looked at your file."

"Exercise is good for my lungs," Stevie said.

"Makes sense," Mia said. "Is that all?"

"One more thing. I don't want anyone to know. I don't want people to feel sorry for me."

Nodding, Mia put her index finger to her lips, indicating that Stevie's secret would be safe. Stevie thanked her and said goodbye. Mia was cool, she thought, walking out of the gym.

It was dusk, and the cold air surprised Stevie with its crisp bite. Around her, the leaves were turning shades of gold. Her footsteps were the only sounds she heard. She thought about her mom, wishing she could be different, less obsessed. Stevie swallowed. A gentle eddy tossed the leaves about. She walked the twelve blocks to the First Bank of Riverdale. Dreading the inevitable confrontation with her mom, Stevie watched the leaves swirl and scatter.

Chapter 6

At lunch time, Stevie grabbed her back-pack and headed for the far right side of the front lawn. This area was informally understood to be the hangout for drama-kids and band members. To the immediate left were the jocks and their cheerleader groupies, and beyond them were the politicos. The cliques and their territories were well established; freshmen were expected to figure it out and respect it.

Stevie spotted Terra, Kyle, Nellie and some of the others already sitting on the lawn, their backpacks strewn across the grass. She said "hello" and sat down with them, and opened her lunch. She hoped no one would notice how awkward she felt. Kyle waved at her, and several others nodded in her direction. Terra didn't acknowledge her presence. Bumming about it wasn't an option — she was way too hungry.

That morning, Stevie had overslept, and had skipped breakfast to get her homework done. She'd grabbed a high calorie shake on the way out, but had forgotten to take her enzymes. Her mom knew she'd be starving by lunch time, so she told Stevie she'd packed more food than usual.

Stevie, grateful, scarfed down a double-decker ham and cheese sandwich, a thermos of split pea soup, a bag of Doritos, an apple and two Twinkies. She polished off a box of chocolate milk and a yogurt drinkable. Finishing, she pulled out enzymes she'd gotten from the nurse. She was about to take them when she noticed Kyle staring.

"Bad headache?" he asked.

"Uh ... they're vitamins," she said, shoving them in her pocket so he couldn't see them. They didn't really look like vitamins.

"I notice you have a delicate appetite," Kyle teased.

Stevie cringed. She'd eaten way more than usual, but even her usual was twice what anyone her age would eat. She had an insatiable appetite. She knew that wasn't uncommon; CF made it almost impossible to digest food without the aid of enzyme supplements. And even with them, it was very difficult to gain weight. Stevie was encouraged to eat a high-calorie diet with unrestricted fat, and had to take enzyme pills with each meal. Stevie's friends who didn't know she had CF resented her for staying so thin.

Stevie tried to look nonchalant as she turned to watch Terra demonstrating proper dance stature to a sophomore who was new to Company. "Take your sternum and pull it up so it's on a 45 degree angle," she said, pointing to the middle of her chest. "That opens you up to the audience and yourself. It frees you, helps you link the movements together."

"We didn't do that when I taught ballet," said Josh, smirking.

"In which lifetime was that?" Terra shot back.

"The one and the present," Josh returned. "I'm an excellent choreographer, you know."

"In your dreams," Terra retorted.

Josh flinched. In rehearsals Stevie had seen he was a natural performer. But he had a limited repertoire. Built like a bean stalk, he didn't seem to know what to do with his arms and hands. Given his gawkiness, Stevie was surprised by his arrogance.

Kyle jumped in. "You do okay."

What a relief that Kyle had joined their conversation and wasn't focusing on her pills! Her mind wandered to the last time she had skipped her enzymes. She'd suffered major stomach pains. Today her lunch had had a lot of fat, which meant it would be riskier than usual not to take them. Was it worth it? Yes, if it meant Kyle wouldn't find out her secret.

"Give 'em what they want," Josh said without modesty. "That's my motto."

A tall girl with short purple hair and dangle earrings was giving advice to a boy named Hale. "Concentrate hard on what you give to your secret buddy because you know they're going to find out who you are. You want them to say, 'Yeah, that was a cool gift.' See these?" she said, pointing to her earrings. "I got them from Nellie two years ago."

A girl with a squeaky voice jumped in. Stevie thought her name might be Erica. "Everyone thought they were fab."

"Yeah, you want to float their boat, give 'em a thrill as they try to figure out who you are," Juliana said.

The bell blared, signaling the end of lunch. Stevie threw the remains of her lunch in the trash. Kyle called after her as she walked away. "See you at rehearsal."

Stevie watched Kyle's casual swagger. What was his motivation for being nice? Did he pity her because no one else seemed to notice she was alive? At that thought, Stevie flinched. But Kyle seemed to be genuinely nice to everyone. With a deep breath, Stevie gathered her books close to her chest. Students were dispersing, heading to their classes. She looked back at the lawn, then quickened her steps as she headed back into the building.

Afternoon homeroom class was really boring.

Her teacher, Mr. Lorenz, gave a lecture on study skills. "By ninth grade, the train is leaving with or without you. If you had trouble last year, you should have taken a class during summer school. If you didn't, you still have an opportunity on Saturday mornings."

Stevie was fidgety. She had left a secret buddy gift for Josh outside his locker and wondered if he would like it. She had agonized to find just the right thing; she wanted to give something clever and personal, but not too intimate. She finally decided on a disposable camera and a note with a double entendre, "To record your best moves."

At rehearsal, Stevie eyed Josh carefully to see if she could gauge his reaction. He seemed happy. Mia suggested that members of Company buy tickets to an avant-garde interpretation of "Romeo and Juliet" that was being performed downtown. According to Mia, the choreography was interesting and the dancing incredible. "Hit your parents up. Get them to take you to as many shows as possible. You might want to consider a part-time job so you can buy your own tickets. Many of you want to be choreographers; each time you see a performance, you'll learn something."

"What about the Fosse show?" Juliana asked.

"Amazing, a must-see. The only negatives are that it's repetitive and a bit too long," Mia said. She clapped her hands. "Time to get up and dance. Put your arms above your head, legs are straight from the hips. Roll down with your elbows, *plié* and up, 5, 6, 7. Contract, round up, contract, then flat back. Lean forward, just your head and shoulders. *Plié* and down, 2, bounce, 2, up slowly, neck is last to come up. *Passé* right leg, 6, and 7, up on 8, *plié* and *relevé*."

On the last *plié* and up, Stevie doubled over as a sudden pain knifed through her stomach. She panicked. Not wanting to disturb the group, she left the studio. Instead of using the gym's bathroom, she ran back to the main building.

Twenty minutes on the toilet surrounded by a very unpleasant odor was a typical CF sentence that was easier to serve in complete privacy. It was 4:00 and most students cleared out of the main building as soon as the 3:14 bell rang.

After Stevie finished in the bathroom, she started back to the studio to pick up her backpack, but decided against getting it. She didn't want to deal with questions. She would have to ask someone from each class for the homework assignments, but it was worth it. Instead, she walked to the curb in front of school, where she had arranged to meet her mom at 4:30.

Her mom pulled up just as Stevie arrived. Stevie said a quick hello and didn't look at her mother as she buckled herself in. This was the day of her postponed appointment and there was no way she could get out of it. When her mom asked questions, she gave the briefest possible answers.

"You seem tense, honey," her mother remarked.

"You and Dr. Bowman are about to shatter my dreams," Stevie said. She knew she sounded angry but she couldn't help herself.

Her mom patted her knee. From then on, she said nothing to Stevie, but their silence was surprisingly comfortable.

Once at the clinic, Stevie got right into a room because it was late in the day. It was small and bare, with only a clinic bed and two chairs. The walls were painted stark white.

Almost immediately, Jenna Motts came in to measure Stevie's height and weight. Jenna was the RN clinical specialist, and Stevie usually liked her optimism and playfulness. Known around clinic as the "body invader," it was Jenna's job to draw blood, give injections and insert culture sticks deep into her young patients' throats. She also administered the oximetry test to measure Stevie's pulse and find out how much oxygen she was taking in. Today the test showed she was operating at her baseline of 95%. Her mother breathed a sigh of relief, as she always did when the number was above 94.

"Don't look so uptight, Mom," Jenna said. Jenna always called Mrs. Jaeger "Mom."

"She's been skipping her mid-day treatment, so I didn't know what to expect," Mrs. Jaeger admitted.

Stevie rolled her eyes. Jenna waited for a moment, eyes on Stevie.

"What about the other two treatments?" Jenna asked.

Stevie's mom looked up, then shrugged helplessly. "She's usually responsible about doing them."

Jenna studied Stevie. "I don't like it when you give me the silent treatment."

Stevie was contrite. "Sorry."

"Are you taking your Ultrase?"

"Never miss," Stevie lied.

Jenna squeezed Stevie's shoulder. "Good. Your sats are fine but we'll talk with the doctor about your protocol. I've got to see the next patient but Lissa will be in soon."

Lissa was the CF social worker. She was a calming presence, and in her own quiet way, always got to the core of the emotional issues that accompanied CF. She greeted Stevie's mom with a hug and then said, "I want a minute alone with Stevie."

"She's not very talkative," her mom said. "Don't think you'll get much out of her."

Stevie hated it when her mom talked about her as if she wasn't there.

"I'll take my chances," Lissa said, and smiled.

When the door clicked shut, Lissa asked Stevie how things were going.

Stevie watched Lissa carefully so she could judge her reaction. She explained that her mother didn't want her to dance in Company. "The point

42

is, I got in. I'm the only freshman," she told Lissa.

"Why is your mom so upset about that?"

Stevie felt a rush of warmth for Lissa, but still, she answered tersely. "Isn't it your job to figure this stuff out?"

"It's harder if you don't tell me."

"Duh. I want to dance with Company."

Lissa nodded. "We can make that happen."

"Not without my mother having a coronary," Stevie said. "Company starts right after school so there isn't time for a mid-day treatment."

"Ay, there's the rub!" Lissa quoted. She thought for a minute, and Stevie panicked. Had she blown it?

Lissa saw Stevie's face and waved her hand, dismissing Stevie's anxiety. "Not to worry, we've got options. Let me talk with Dr. Bowman." She left her alone for a short while. When she was gone, Stevie imagined what Dr. Bowman might say: maybe, "Stick with your old routine; it's working," or "Can't you go 30 minutes late?" This, of course, would be impossible.

Stevie was lost in negative thoughts when Dr. Bowman walked in. A very tall man with distinguished gray hair and blue eyes, he had his own uniform — khaki pants and a solid color polo shirt. Stevie was comfortable with Dr. Bowman. Little kids liked him, too, she knew. He always said, "Kids are incredible. One minute you can poke them with a needle and the next minute they're pulling on your tie or playing with your stethoscope."

Dr. Bowman was holding her chart, jotting notes while he spoke, "I wish all your problems were this easy to solve."

Stevie gripped the metal rim of her seat, afraid of getting her hopes up.

"We're going to get you a Flutter," Dr. Bowman said, rummaging through a cabinet, "Here we go." He held up what looked like a white bubble pipe. The top screwed off the chamber. Inside was a heavy metal ball. "This device allows you to loosen and eliminate mucus from your airways," he explained.

The respiratory therapist walked in as Dr. Bowman was talking. His name was Jimmy Ross. The first time Stevie had seen him, his deep bellowing voice had scared her. But once she'd gotten to know him, she discovered he was really kind. Stevie had grown to love his corny jokes and his musical laughter.

"Hey sweetie," Jimmy said. "How have you been?"

"Okay," Stevie said, forcing a smile. She was skeptical of the Flutter. Yet another way to do airway clearance.

"You're going to love this thing once you see how easy it is," Jimmy promised, "Check this out." Jimmy slowly inhaled. He continued to inhale beyond what looked like a normal breath.

"It's tricky," Dr. Bowman said. "You need to take in quite a bit of air, but don't fill your lungs all the way up." As he spoke, Jimmy put the Flutter in his mouth, and waited two or three seconds. Then he exhaled, fast but not forcefully.

"It's your turn," said Dr. Bowman, taking out another Flutter for Stevie.

While Stevie inhaled, Jimmy told her to think about what she was doing. "Visualize your airways vibrating and the mucus being loosened and propelled along. Exhale from your smaller to your larger airways. Cough it out."

Stevie coughed up quite a bit of phlegm. She was repulsed. "Very attractive," she said. Even at clinic she was capable of feeling embarrassed.

Dr. Bowman ignored Stevie. "By blowing into the Flutter, you see, you'll start the ball vibrating. These vibrations resonate down the airways, causing the airway walls to vibrate. It has other advantages as well."

"Name one," Stevie challenged.

Dr. Bowman was matter of fact. "It's portable ... fits in your backpack. Doesn't require another person the way CPT does."

"It's funny-looking," Stevie said, not wanting to admit that this might be the answer to her prayers.

"It solves the problem of that intrusive mid-day treatment," Dr. Bowman continued. "Ten minutes right after school. No need to go home for CPT."

Stevie turned the Flutter over in her hand. "Looks like we've got a sale," said Jimmy.

45

"Not quite," Stevie mumbled. "You still need to convince my mom."

Dr. Bowman smiled. "Three against one. She doesn't stand a chance."

Chapter 7

Stevie was nervous about returning to Company the next day. Leaving early without explanation was bound to elicit curiosity. Especially since someone might have noticed that she left her backpack against the front wall.

When Mia returned, she winked at Stevie and launched into a discussion of protocol for people auditioning their own choreography. "I don't expect a finished dance so don't be nervous about that. It would be helpful if you tell me a little about your piece ... what you have in mind ... where you're going with it. Remember, the choreography doesn't have to tell a story, but you should be trying to communicate something."

Coming up for air, Mia granted a five minute respite. As Company members were going for water and candy bars, she walked over to Stevie and asked her to stay during break. "Is everything okay?"

"Stomach problems. I'm better now."

"Glad to hear it," Mia sounded genuine. "I want you to know I'm here if you need me."

Stevie was grateful for Mia's kindness.

After the break, Mia read the names of the three dances she would audition that day. "RapCity" was up first. "It's a three-section piece," said Heather, turning on a tape of bluesy music by John Coltrane. She and Josh, dressed in pajamas, faced each other in mirror image and took up both sides of the makeshift stage. Their movements were a slow duet of waking up and getting ready for work. All of the choreography was symmetrical, and within two minutes, they had put on full suits, overcoats and hats, and were carrying briefcases.

Stevie was mesmerized by how real it was. Although the dance was clearly meant to be fun, it reminded her of when her father used to get ready for work, and she ached with longing. He had died of a heart attack five years before, and Stevie still missed him very much.

Part two of "RapCity" took place in the city itself, and began with a series of abstract modern steps set to Billy Joel's "Running On Ice." Other dancers played various parts — a woman being tugged by an imaginary dog on a leash, two robbers with flashlights and face masks, and a boy who needed a crutch to walk.

The next sequence was done with an element of slapstick. Two businessmen were being attacked by the robbers when a police officer arrived on the scene. A chase ensued, and the robbers ran off. Company members laughed at the comic touch.

For the last section, John Coltrane was back on as the two disheveled businessmen arrived home. Heather and Josh cleaned each other up, prepared their supper, and went to bed. Everyone clapped when they were finished.

Terra's "Black Widow" was next. She said she and Kyle were dancing the story of an insect who falls in love with a spider. She'd been inspired by the dark sensuality of the music, a song called "Group Four" by Massive Attack.

In the beginning, the mother spider spun a web to trap the insect. A courtship of sorts began, as a power struggle ensued between the spider and the insect. The spider triumphed because her poison was stronger than his. The insect was left dying as the mother collected her children. They crawled off, the mother spinning another web for future prey.

As the spider, Terra was sensual and lithe, and her movements easily suggested the power and allure of a black widow. Kyle's movements were strong and sinewy, his performance dark and foreboding. Company loved their performance and went wild when they finished, issuing forth with applause, whistles and cheers. Flushed and satisfied, Terra curtsied like a real ballerina.

After Terra and Kyle finished, Juliana Henderson stood up. She explained that the Troop, the Cabbage Patch, the Snake and Roger Rabbit were old dance steps from the early 80s that were making a comeback. She did a routine to a remix of hip-hop, with six other dancers that included other, more contemporary steps. Interspersed were some suggestive moves that drew Mia's disapproval.

"The trend in dancing is incredibly nasty." Mia said. "Even ten and twelve year olds are moving in inappropriate ways. The entire faculty will be sitting in the front row and my job will be on the line if I let you do your dance. It's out of the question."

"Is any of it salvageable?" Juliana asked.

Mia ignored the question. "Laura will be first tomorrow."

"She should know better," Kyle whispered to Stevie.

Terra raised her hand and asked if they could discuss the poster that would publicize the concert. Traditionally, it featured only the senior soloist, although some years it was done with two or three dancers. It was a considerable honor to be selected.

"It's too early to decide," replied Mia. "We don't even know whether the featured piece will be a solo or a duet."

Heather rolled her eyes. Everyone knew Terra had been groomed to dance the featured piece. How silly of Mia to pretend it wasn't already a *fait accompli*. But if Mia wanted to play it that way, so be it.

"Regardless of who does it, I have a concept," Terra ventured.

Mia peered over her glasses. "Let's hear it."

"We see the back of a torso. A solo female figure stands against a completely black background. She's naked but we only see her as luminescent. Very dramatic."

Mia shook her head. "No way. Completely inappropriate."

"It's merely suggestive," Terra countered.

"The faculty won't go for it." Mia was firm.

"I just don't understand what you're afraid of," Terra challenged.

"You don't have to understand what I'm afraid of. You just have to understand the word 'no,'" Mia said.

Josh smirked. "Little Miss Diva doesn't like the word 'no.'"

Kyle stood up and addressed Mia. "We know how you work. By now you probably have the whole concept in mind, even if some of the details are fuzzy. I'll bet everyone here wants to know what you're thinking."

Stevie adored Kyle's candor. It was obvious that the rest of Company did too, as murmurs of approval circulated through the room. Mia must have felt ambivalent about his direct approach. Her face was a complicated mesh of expressions that included grudging admiration as well as mild anger for being publicly crossed.

"There's a funky-looking girl in a midriff top and jeans," Mia began. "She's kneeling in a hip street pose. She holds her hand out and we see a shot of a classical ballerina in a tutu, arms overhead, leg in front *attitude*. The picture of the ballerina is in miniature and placed in the hand of the street girl. That's the shot."

"There's nothing provocative about it," Terra protested.

"It represents what I'm looking for in our concert," Mia said, evenly. "Hip-hop meets ballet *en pointe*. We're minimizing the rules represented by the ballerina and emphasizing the freedom of attitude. The freedom is holding the rules. I think the student body will like it."

"So, hypothetically speaking, if I'm the soloist, I'll be the little ballerina?"

"No. If you're the soloist, I'll put you in the midriff. That's provocative, isn't it?"

There was a moment of silence. Terra would not admit it, but she loved the idea.

Chapter 8

Ugh! Look at my legs. I'm so fat!" Terra complained to Heather as other Company members plunked down for the Monday meeting. Mia hadn't arrived, as evidenced by the incredibly high noise level.

"Don't start," said Julie, rolling her eyes.

"I am." Terra grabbed some flesh from her hips.

Stevie spoke without thinking. "That's muscle. You need it to dance."

"Then how do you manage, Little Miss Size Zero?" Terra's sarcasm wounded Stevie.

Kyle drew an imaginary arrow across a bow and shot it into Stevie's heart to indicate the pain Terra's words had inflicted. Then he pulled Stevie aside. "Ignore her, she's just jealous." Stevie felt her heart pounding as Kyle came to her rescue. "You're a perfect size two," he remarked. Stevie didn't feel like a perfect anything, but refrained from saying so.

Mia walked in. Coincidentally, she took up the subject of weight as she sat the dancers down. "I'm hearing a lot of talk about dieting this year," Mia began. "Watching your weight is okay, but you need to keep your motor running. Eat healthy, well-balanced meals. Lots of protein, carbs, fruits and vegetables. But remember, you're going to be on-stage in a unitard. So skip the dessert and watch your fats."

Stevie had heard that some years Company was comprised of eaters and other years its members were compulsive dieters. She thought it was weird that a group could collectively become weight-obsessed. While she pondered this concept, Mia rambled on about good eating habits, emphasizing the color of food as an important criterion.

Oranges and yellows are good for vitamin A, she explained, naming butternut squash, carrots, cantaloupe, citrus fruits and mangoes as key examples. In the dark greens category, brussels sprouts, broccoli and dark lettuce worked best, she said. Raspberries, strawberries, peppers and tomatoes — any of the reds and pinks — were also helpful. Equally important, she urged, was keeping up with schoolwork and maintaining a 2.0 grade point average. The threat loomed large for all of them. "If you don't," she warned, "you won't dance in our concert."

The next thing she said stayed with Stevie. "Some of the relationships you make here will last forever. A lot of my former students tell me they have never been as close to anybody as they were to their fellow Company members. Don't take each other for granted."

Stevie was putting books in her locker when Clara asked if she wanted to make their monthly run to Paradise Thrift on Saturday. "It's the first of the month, remember?"

Stevie frowned. "I can't. I have rehearsal."

"You're so busy these days," Clara said sadly.

Stevie knew Clara was unhappy about her schedule, and felt guilty that she didn't have much time for her old friend. But she was so busy these days with Company rehearsals. Trying to be kind, she attempted to hide her overwhelming sense of pride. "Saturdays are out until concert is over. I know it seems like I'm not very available, but second semester all my Saturdays are free."

Clara remained silent and continued to sort through the books in her locker. After a pause she drew in her breath. "Can I get you anything while I'm there?"

Stevie shook her head no. She needed to save her money for the dance convention in Palm Springs and said so.

"I hear they have a great outlet mall there,"

Clara said wistfully.

Stevie shrugged her shoulders. "I'll let you know. They're posting which pieces got into concert. I've got to go."

Stevie started off.

"Wait a sec," Clara called after her. "Can you come over tonight so we can study for our English test?"

"No way," Stevie answered. "Rehearsal won't end until 6:00. And then I've got to do treatment. It'll be too late."

Chapter 9

Everyone was on pins and needles waiting for Mia to announce which dances had been chosen. Stevie turned to Heather and said, "I haven't gotten anything from my secret buddy yet."

"You'll get something, you've just got to be patient," Heather answered.

Before Mia named the pieces, she revealed that Terra and Stevie were going to be in the poster. The photo shoot would be on Tuesday after school. Terra didn't look the least bit surprised; Stevie almost hyperventilated.

Fortunately, Mia segued right into a discussion of the selection process. "I want to reassure you that all of the pieces were good. In the end, I simply had to make some choices. If I didn't, the concert would be four hours long."

Stevie saw how calm the experienced dancers like Terra and Kyle were. What a contrast to some of the newer members, who were abuzz with nerves!

"Can you just ... get on with it?" a voice called out from the back of the room. Stevie craned her neck to see who had been so bold, but she couldn't tell.

"I suppose I've stalled long enough. 'Caffeine Jitters — Good Morning L.A.,' 'RapCity,' 'Bring It On,' 'Black Widow,' 'No More Mr. Nice Guy,' and 'Computer Games' are in. 'It Don't Mean A Thing' will be the full Company finale," Mia said. Suddenly, the room could be divided between the ecstatic and the devastated. In the latter category, some were in tears, while others only looked sullen. A few were doing their best to feign indifference.

"You all have the option of trying again next year," Mia said encouragingly. "I suspect that since you'll be working with more seasoned choreographers during the year, your approaches will be more sophisticated the next time you audition. I can't make any promises, but you'll undoubtedly have a better shot."

Mia's words were of little comfort to those who had been rejected. She offered up a box of tissues and told everyone to pull themselves together.

"Are we gonna dance today?" Laura asked.

"Yes. We're doing a workshop on counterbalance," Mia confirmed. "But before we begin, I want to announce that Stevie will be Terra's understudy."

Stevie gasped.

"It's an honor to be an understudy but it's also a huge commitment." Mia was unapologetic. "You are required to be at every rehearsal and you must know the material backwards and forwards."

Stevie was tentative. "Will I get a chance to perform?"

"No. You'll own the dance but never have an audience unless something happens to Terra. That's what it means to be an understudy," Mia stated flatly. "Two minutes and then we'll begin."

Terra turned to Stevie, smirking. "Don't count on it."

Stevie didn't care. She would become Terra's shadow; she'd copy her every move. What an incredible experience, she thought. "Will Kyle rehearse with both of us?" she asked Terra.

"What difference does it make?" Terra replied. "You'd only be wasting his time. You're never going to dance my part. The only reason you're the understudy is because all the good dancers are in other numbers."

Once again, Stevie was stung by Terra's words, but she was determined to earn Terra's respect. She measured out her words. "I hope you'll have a better opinion of my dancing after wc've worked together."

"We'll never work together," Terra shot back. "You'll always work under me." She sauntered over to Juliana and Heather.

Stevie gritted her teeth. I will win her over, she told herself, even if it kills me! As she was plotting her strategy, the room grew suddenly darker. Music from the speakers boomed out, and a man was chanting to a background of repetitive bells. It was very New Age, and it quickly changed the mood in the room.

"The philosophy of counter-balance is that your weight and that of another person can support each other," said Mia. "Please pair up according to your size. Two girls who weigh roughly the same should work together. The same goes for the guys."

Everyone looked around and tried to find someone similar in stature. Stevie, hugely self-conscious, was much shorter and lighter than anyone else. She hung back and waited to see who was left.

Mia scanned the room. "Who doesn't have a partner?"

Stevie raised her hand tentatively.

"Come help me demonstrate," Mia motioned her to the front of the room. "Stevie and I aren't the same size." There was laughter all around at the obviousness of this statement. "Once you master this technique, you don't need to be." She stood with her feet apart. "Join your right hands together with outstretched arms. Both of you should keep your feet firmly planted and lean away from each other."

"If one partner lets go," Mia warned, "both will fall down." She told everyone to bend their knees and sink closer to the ground. "Try to get used to each other's weight by going up and down. Use your partner's weight to keep yourself suspended."

Throughout the room, the dancers followed Mia's instructions.

"She's too heavy. I keep falling," Juliana cried out. "How can I stay up?"

"If you're lighter, you need to lean farther back." As Mia continued, many of them dropped out. "Trust is a big part of this. It's hard to allow someone to hold your weight. One of you should keep your legs firmly planted while your partner extends their leg behind them in *arabesque*."

Offering her right arm to Stevie, Mia pulled her in as they both faced the class. Mia bent her knees and put her hips under Stevie's torso, holding on to her shoulders. Stevie felt herself lifted off the ground and turned around. With Mia, Stevie could be completely trusting, and she extended her torso in an extreme angle.

"Are you ready to do me?" Mia asked.

Nodding, Stevie bent her knees and used the power of her legs to push Mia's body up above her. Because of her size, she had to push herself way back in an awkward angle to support Mia.

Mia extended her left leg and turned, using Stevie as her prop. "The reason Stevie is able to hold my weight is because she is using counterbalance." Turning to Stevie she said, "You're a natural."

All eyes in the room were focused on Stevie. She overheard Terra, who was standing next to Kyle, murmur, "She's okay." Stevie flushed with pleasure. As she put Mia down, Stevie started coughing.

"Good job, Stevie. I'll see you all tomorrow," Mia said, and dismissed the class. Stevie's coughs continued and became more violent, bringing mucus from her lungs into her throat. She knew she should get the phlegm out of her system, but she was way too embarrassed to spit it out in front of the class. It was disgusting to swallow that gunk, but she had no choice. She waited until the coughing subsided.

"Are you okay?" Megan asked.

"Maybe you should get some water," Laura suggested.

"I'm fine." Stevie wished everyone would drop the subject.

"She needs an Ice Blended." Kyle was definitive. "I'm taking her to the Tea Leaf."

In spite of herself, Stevie was euphoric. Kyle was taking her out.

Kyle gathered his stuff and tossed Stevie her backpack. Turning to the others, Kyle cupped his hands and yelled, "Anyone interested, meet at the Tea Leaf on Forest Drive in 15 minutes."

Instantly crushed, Stevie silently berated herself. How naïve she was to think that Kyle could be interested in her. Still, being with him in a group was better than not being with him at all. She opened her backpack and looked at the Flutter, knowing it was time to do a treatment. Immediately, she closed it back up. Treatment would just have to wait.

"Are you coming?" Kyle asked Terra.

Terra looked at Stevie. "Pass."

After Terra left, Kyle put his arm around Stevie's shoulders. "You want to dance like her. She wants to be skinny like you," he said.

Stevie wondered if this was really true. It could be, she thought. How perceptive Kyle was. He was so amazing! Afraid her attraction would show in her eyes, Stevie looked down.

"Let's walk," Kyle suggested. He picked up Stevie's backpack and slung it over his shoulder.

At the Tea Leaf, Kyle ordered a Vanilla Ice Blended for himself and Stevie asked for a Mocha. Waiting for the drinks, Kyle chatted up the girl behind the counter as Stevie stood by, silently wishing she could think of something witty to say. Clusters of other dancers were already deep in conversation. She waited until they were seated to strike up a conversation. "So what do you do when you're not dancing?"

"I have a lot of creative outlets; writing songs is one of them," said Kyle. "It's a great way to get my feelings out. And I love to read. How about you?"

"I like to read, too," she said. Not only was Kyle handsome, she thought, he was articulate and literate. She tried to find the right words, wanting desperately to sound older than 14. "Maya Angelou is amazing. *I Know Why the Caged Bird Sings* is my favorite."

"She's awesome," Kyle murmured approvingly. Just then, he reached into his pockets and pulled out a cigarette. Stevie almost died. Having CF made second-hand smoke a major taboo. Kyle flagged down an employee for a light. Leaning back, he took a puff and then turned his head slightly so he wouldn't release smoke in Stevie's direction. But even the small amount of smoke that came Stevie's way was enough to elicit a cough. She covered her mouth and struggled to stifle it.

The thought crossed Stevie's mind that this minimal exposure might hurt her already damaged lungs. She felt vulnerable, wondering if all the things Dr. Bowman had told her about smoking were true. Was second-hand smoke really an irritant? Could the tar get stuck in her lungs if she didn't actually smoke the cigarette herself? Maybe not, who knows?

And then there was her mother. What would she think? Stevie knew the answer; her mother would have a heart attack if she saw her.

Chapter 10

The photo shoot was scheduled for Tuesday after school. Terra walked in wearing a revealing red and black fish-net top over a black bra and black shorts. Seeing her, Nellie squealed, "Ooh la la!" and backed away, laughing. Josh whistled and chuckled.

"Wow!" Heather said.

Mia shot Terra a disapproving look.

"You were right, Mia," Kyle howled. "It is provocative."

Mia reprimanded Terra. "I said midriff, not bra top."

"Are you going to make me change?" she asked.

"In a word, yes," Mia said, handing Terra a crop top.

Terra shrugged resignedly and walked to the

corner to change. When she came back, she brushed by Stevie, who was dressed in a pink classical ballerina costume and toe shoes. Stevie moved aside, feeling awkwardly overdressed next to the other kids' sweatpants and T-shirts. She was alternately proud and embarrassed. Chosen because of her size, she was still the only freshman ever to be picked for the poster.

"How can she put a freshman in the poster?" Nellie asked.

Josh answered immediately. "Stevie is the smallest in Company."

Heather protested. "She's an apprentice. She isn't really in Company."

Terra gave a smirk. "Doesn't matter. It's perfect. She'll be in the palm of my hand so I can crush her any time I want."

The group laughed. Stevie wondered whether she would survive until the concert. It was tradition to haze freshmen, she knew, but she'd expected only a few harmless pranks. Getting dissed in front of everyone was another story.

Terra modeled the more conservative top, sticking out her tongue to poke fun as she did. The photographer, who doubled as the makeup artist, was a middle-aged man named Jim. He signaled to Terra when it was time to get her face painted.

Jim went for a smoldering look, applying a shimmery dark blue eye shadow all over the top lid and then sweeping it under the bottom lashes.

To create a pouty look around the mouth, he lined her lips with a bronze-colored pencil one shade darker than her lipstick.

The pose Jim wanted for Terra was what Mia had initially suggested. He got her to crouch low and hold her hand out, palm up. Against a dark backdrop, Jim snapped several rolls of film and said Terra was a natural in front of the camera. He asked her to improvise, and she thrust her hip out. He suggested a few other poses, all the while snapping shot after shot.

Stevie watched all of this with trepidation. It seemed unfair that anyone could be so comfortable with such an inordinate amount of attention being lavished upon her.

"You're up," Jim said, pointing at Stevie.

Terra went and sat down with Heather and Juliana. "I can't wait to see this."

Brushing Stevie's hair back from her forehead, Jim pinned it in a classic bun, creating the look of a ballerina. He dusted a pale pink blush onto the apples of her cheeks and, to play up her brown eyes, swept light eyeshadow into the creases of her lids, sweeping it up and out towards her brows. He filled in her brows with a golden-brown pencil. The final touch was a raspberry-toned lip gloss. When he was finished, she looked like a pink princess.

Josh moseyed up to Stevie and curtsied in front of her. "Lovely, your highness," he said in falsetto.

"Ah, you like my work," said Jim.

Stevie didn't know what to say.

Jim continued to tinker with the lighting. He changed the filter so the backdrop was much lighter and told Stevie to pose *en pointe*, arms overhead, with her leg in *attitude devant*. She was nervous but she got through the photo shoot without incident. When she finished, she packed up her gym bag.

Mia walked over to where Terra was sitting. "Great job today. You looked really good," Mia said to her. "Your weight seems to be under control. You're now a lean, mean, dancing machine."

"I'm loving this," Terra admitted.

"I don't want you to lose any more weight."

Terra chirped. "You can never be too rich or too thin."

"Maybe, if you're in the New York City Ballet Company." Mia's tone was sharp. "But no one really wants to look at those skeletons."

Terra crossed her arms defensively and pointed at Stevie. "She's way skinnier than I am, and you don't have a problem with her."

Stevie felt her cheeks burn.

Mia was emphatic. "You have totally different body types."

"I have to lose weight if I'm going to dance professionally," Terra reminded her.

"I know that. But if you lose it too fast, it won't stay off. And I don't want you to get too weak." Mia glanced at her watch and realized it was time to dismiss everyone. "We'll continue this conversation another time."

Stevie went to her locker. To her surprise, she saw a wrapped package on the bench in front of it. There was a card taped to it that read, "Dear Stevie, It's time to dress for success. From your secret buddy." Stevie tore the package open, excited to see what her first gift was.

Pulling out a training bra, Stevie was horrified. She quickly shoved it into her gym bag, glancing around to see if anyone else had seen it. Fortunately, she was alone. Stevie had to lean against the wall in the hallway to steady herself. It was hard enough dealing with her own feelings about being flat-chested, but being mocked about it was unbearably painful. How many people were in on this, she wondered. The question would haunt her all day.

That night, her mom knocked on Stevie's bedroom door. She wanted to say goodnight. Stevie was staring at her body in the mirror.

"What's wrong?" her mother asked.

Stevie wilted. "I hate my body."

"You're supposed to hate your body. You're 14."

"I have a serious figure flaw! I'm the only one my age who doesn't have ... " Stevie groped for the right word. " ... a bustline," she finished, weakly.

"Dr. Bowman says it happens later for

teenagers with CF."

"How much later?" Stevie demanded.

Her mom didn't answer. "What about getting a bra and stuffing it? We used to do that."

Stevie walked over to her dresser and pulled out the training bra she had shoved in the bottom drawer. "What do you suggest I use? Toilet paper?"

"Where did you get that?"

Stevie told her mom about finding the bra, and the note that came with it. Her mother wanted to know why someone would give her a gift like that. Stevie explained the secret buddy program.

"How could Mia let that happen? This can't be what she had in mind!"

Stevie softened. "Mia doesn't get to decide which gifts are exchanged."

"It's her program, so she's responsible. I'm calling her right now."

"Mom, no," Stevie pleaded. "It's embarrassing enough."

"I'll make sure she handles it in a way that doesn't hurt you."

"Too late for that," Stevie said resignedly. She was terrified.

Chapter 11

Mia did not look happy. "Time for everyone to sit down," she said. "We need to have a short meeting before we dance."

Stevie's heart skipped a beat. Mia had reassured her mom she would handle things without compromising Stevie but she hadn't given her any details. Mia waited for everyone to settle down before she began.

"Company is like a family. We spend as much time together as you probably do with your real families. You need to be kind to each other. And you need to be respectful ... of each other ... and of me."

Murmurs came from around the room, as no one was sure where Mia was going with this.

"You need to be on time. You need to pay attention. You need to keep your voices down.

Many of you are not ready for rehearsals when you do get here. And you're sharing clothes, which is not okay. All of this will change."

Mia stopped and looked around the room. There was dead silence and all eyes were upon her.

She continued. "No one is allowed to wear what he or she wore to school. I want you to change into appropriate dance clothing before you show up here and be ready to go at 3:20. If you don't, I'll make the girls wear black leotards and tights, and the boys wear sweats and plain white T-shirts."

Company members grumbled. Mia talked over their discontent. "Lots of the dances have too many people. If you're not paying attention during rehearsal, you're out. If there are only a few dancers and someone messes up, that person will be replaced. We have a big Company this year. There are plenty of people in line to take your place."

Holding up the training bra that Stevie had received, Mia stared them down. "And now we're going to talk about this. One of you gave this to your secret buddy. I find it appalling. Secret buddies are supposed to make you feel warm and fuzzy, not create stress or bad feelings."

Mia paused for emphasis. "This is an inappropriate gift. You should only be giving gifts that you would be comfortable letting your mother see. Whoever gave this needs to come forward, take responsibility, and apologize."

After she stopped talking, no one moved a muscle. Minutes ticked by, and people started fidgeting, looking at each other to see if the culprit would confess. Mia wagged her finger at the group. "No one is going anywhere until I get to the bottom of this."

Finally, Terra stood up, quavering. "It was a joke. I was trying to trick my secret buddy. Make her think I didn't like her. But I was going to shower her with great gifts tomorrow. I already bought ... "

Mia interrupted her. "That's nothing short of cruel. You should be ashamed of yourself."

Terra stood paralyzed. Mia pressed for an answer but she said nothing. There was an awkward silence as everyone waited for a response. Several more minutes passed before Terra apologized.

"I'm really sorry, Stevie," she said.

Summoning her courage, Stevie stood up and looked Terra in the eye. She forced herself to ignore everyone except Terra. "Some girls might have been offended by this, but I know you didn't mean any harm. The funny thing is, I don't even need it yet. I took this as a sign you're rooting for me."

Everyone laughed at Stevie's response. Terra flashed a grateful smile.

"You're lucky that Stevie is so forgiving," Mia said. "But I'm going on record right here and now. The secret buddy program will be over, and the offender will be kicked out of Company, if I ever see or hear about a malicious gift again. End of discussion. Time to break into your rehearsal groups."

Terra walked over to Stevie. "Thanks for being so cool."

"You didn't leave me much choice," Stevie admitted. "I can't stand to be pitied."

Stevie felt Terra looking at her as if appraising her. "Can we get a soda after rehearsal?" Terra asked.

Stevie stopped. "Sure," she said. This major breakthrough was tempered only by the thought that her mom would kill her for not coming straight home after rehearsal for homework and treatment. But Stevie had her priorities.

At the Tea Leaf, Terra ordered an herb tea for herself and a soda for Stevie. She insisted on paying, and asked Stevie to get a table. While she was waiting for Terra, Stevie rummaged through her purse for her lipstick and felt her fingers on her Flutter. She experienced a sudden pang of guilt, and told herself that she'd have her mom do an extra long session of CPT as soon as she got home.

Terra came breezing over to the table. "Ooh! Great color on your lips. Care to share?"

"Naturalistic's Lip Waves Marbleized Lip Gloss." Stevie said. "The name's a mouthful but "you get two colors swirled into one pot."

"You're pretty savvy about this stuff," Terra said.

"Being so small makes me look really young. Makeup helps."

"I've seen you eat. But you never gain weight," Terra said. "I want to know your secret."

Stevie thought about taking Terra into her confidence. She opened her mouth to speak but then changed her mind. She didn't want to win Terra's favor out of pity. "You have a really good body, Terra."

Terra shook her head. "I'm not thin enough to dance professionally."

They talked for a while and then Terra looked at her watch. "Uh-oh! I've got to get home. My mom's a drill sergeant. Has been ever since my dad left."

"Do you miss him?" Stevie asked.

"I don't miss their fighting." Terra hesitated. "Do you get along with your dad?"

"He died when I was nine."

Terra put her arm around Stevie's shoulders. "I guess neither one of us will be dancing at any father-daughter balls, huh?" she said, smiling sadly.

"Guess not," Stevie said and, in spite of herself, grinned back.

The sky was gray. Rain clouds hovered just

above the skyline, but they didn't dampen Stevie's spirits as she walked home.

Her mother chided her when she walked in the door. "You're late. We should get started right away on your treatment."

All of a sudden, Stevie didn't feel like doing her treatment. She wanted to relish her victory with Terra. Stevie felt her eyelashes twitch. "I just used my Flutter," she said to her mom.

Watching her mom sauté onions, Stevie sat at the kitchen table, pretending to do her algebra homework. She hated lying. But having CF was becoming a major hassle.

Chapter 12

The garage sale was well under way when Josh's mom dropped off fried chicken and corn on the cob for lunch. Most of the kids gnawed on chicken bones and corn cobs, then tossed the remains into a plastic garbage bag. Heather, Juliana and Laura sat on the red and white checked tablecloth that Mia had laid on the ground, and wrestled with their chicken with plastic forks and knives. Josh handed out water bottles while Kyle passed around a box of chocolates he'd brought.

Mia and Nellie were helping customers as Stevie ate, scarfing down seconds of both chicken and corn. When she was completely stuffed, she walked over to a rack of clothing and hid behind it so she could sneak her enzymes. Out of the corner of her eye, she saw Terra re-folding a plaid flannel work-shirt. It struck Stevie as odd that Terra wasn't taking a break for lunch. She walked over to Terra. "Can I make you a plate?" she asked.

"No thanks," Terra said. She quickly held up an old pair of pedal pushers. "These are cool. Do you want to try them on?"

"If you like them, you should get them," Stevie urged. "You spotted them first."

"They're way to small for me. You have to be petite, like you, to look good in them."

Mia eyed Terra suspiciously. "Is that why you aren't eating? Are you trying to cut back?"

"It doesn't hurt to skip a meal like this. Fried chicken and chocolate are loaded with fat."

"Then how about a piece of corn?"

Terra put an end to the discussion. "Pass."

Kyle came up behind them. "Some of us haven't had a break yet," he said, and asked Terra and Stevie if they wanted to take a walk. Terra jumped at the chance, eager to get away from the subject of food. Stevie followed along. When they were a block away, Kyle pulled out a cigarette and lit up. Stevie felt upset and confused, but she kept quiet.

They walked along, Terra buzzing about hairstyles. "You can do a French twist by pulling your hair into a vertical cylinder that you create by twisting the hair and spiraling it down."

"Hence the name," Kyle added.

"It would look fab on Stevie," Terra said.

"I tried something similar once, but it didn't work," Stevie admitted.

Terra scrunched up her nose and giggled. She threw one arm over Kyle's shoulders and ran her other hand through his hair. "Maybe we should try it out on you!"

Stevie felt a pang of jealousy as Terra teased him. They rounded the corner just as Alex, the teller at her mom's bank, was walking his wheaten terrier.

"Stevie, hi," he said with a smile. "You look great."

"Thanks," said Stevie. She bent over to pet George, then asked Alex, "How have you been?"

"No complaints. Actually, I do have one. You haven't been in to see me in a long time."

"I've been busy with the dance company at my high school. That reminds me ... these are two of the dancers. Kyle Matthews and Terra Reede, Alex Callahan."

"Nice to meet you both," said Alex turning towards them. As he did, he saw Kyle's cigarette. In an angry tone he said, "I can't believe you're letting this guy blow smoke in your face."

Kyle got defensive. "I'm not blowing smoke in anyone's face. Besides, we're outside. It dissipates. You didn't even know I was smoking until you saw the cigarette."

"I guess you haven't told him," Alex said sadly.

"Told me what?" Kyle demanded.

79

Stevie quickly extended her arms and gave Alex a big bear hug. "It's great to see you," she said. With one arm she grabbed Kyle, with the other, Terra. "Come on guys, we've got to get back and find out how much money we made." As she whisked them away, Stevie saw Alex out of the corner of her eye, standing there shaking his head.

When Stevie, Kyle and Terra got back to the garage sale, Mia was counting the money. "Looks like we made about $600. It'll cover the strobe lighting I want for concert."

Kyle beamed, high-fiving Stevie and Terra.

At school the next day, Stevie was perched on the railing of a staircase, talking to Victoria, when Clara walked up. "How was the garage sale?" she asked.

"We made $632," Stevie said with pride. She pointed to her pedal pushers. "I got these for three bucks."

Clara's eyes widened. "That's cheaper than Paradise Thrift."

The bell rang. Victoria said good-bye and walked to class. Clara started to leave but Stevie put her hand on Clara's arm. "You should have come!"

"You obviously forgot," Clara chided her. "My parents dragged me to see my great-aunt Betsy. But I'm desperate for some new stuff. Let's go to Paradise Thrift this weekend."

Stevie was apologetic. "I've got the dance convention in Palm Springs." She knew Clara would not be happy about this.

"I'm going to miss you," Clara said sadly. "Call me when you're down there."

"I will," Stevie promised.

The next morning, Stevie bounced down the stairs. She had to be at school by 6:50 since Mia had said the bus to Palm Springs would leave promptly at 7:00. "Mom, I'm ready."

Her mom walked in from the kitchen. "Did you take your meds?"

"I will when I get there."

"I know you're too rushed to do a full treatment, but take ten minutes and do your Flutter before you go."

Stevie pursed her lips. "I don't have time. It will get done. I promise."

Her mom frowned, but let it go. She left the room. In a moment she came back with a bag of snacks. "Just in case," she said with a smirk.

Stevie hugged her. "You're the best, Mom," she said, and resolved to do her Flutter as soon as she got to Palm Springs.

It was some kind of miracle that Stevie's mother had allowed her to attend. It meant skipping nine consecutive chest percussion therapy treatments. Stevie had promised to use her Flutter three times a day and to take Albuterol through an inhaler. Her mom had asked if there would be time to do her treatments. Stevie had reassured her that it would be no problem to go a little late to dinner and get up a bit earlier in the morning.

They were staying at the Riviera Hotel, five minutes away from the convention center. Each hotel room was booked with two double beds so four girls or four boys could stay in each room. During the day they would dance in master classes with 20 school groups from all over the state. Evening programs were scheduled for both nights since Mia considered them to be necessary for the bonding that was an important element of the convention.

And then there was after hours. Kyle had told her it was tradition to sneak out after curfew for some individual bonding. Stevie had felt like he was flirting with her. But then again, he flirted with everyone, particularly Terra. Stevie knew Kyle didn't have a girlfriend, but she wondered if he was secretly interested in someone.

Stevie checked into her room and found that she'd been assigned to share with Heather, Laura and Juliana.

"We're going to slumber in style," Juliana said when she opened up the cabinet and saw the TV on a swivel shelf.

The first class on Friday started promptly at 1:00. It began with a 30 minute warm-up that included an initial sequence of stretches on the floor. Then the class progressed with *pliés* and legwork, *tendue* combinations, *degagés*, and *developés*. Center floor concluded with an *adagio* and small jumps. The dancers then did across-the-floor combinations: *pirouettes*, *chenés*, *piqué* turns, footwork patterns, and *grand jetés*. It was clear throughout the class that Terra had a special gift. Even though she had placed herself amidst the students, she emerged as the leader, with dancers instinctively following her tempos. It was partly her sense of rhythm, partly her technique. Stevie was in awe of her talent.

At 10:30 on Friday night, the phone rang in Stevie's room. Terra was calling to invite Stevie to come over to paint their nails. Terra's room-mates were skipping out to meet some friends from a neighboring school. Terra told Stevie she wanted to experiment with some makeup since the guy she had her eye on wasn't showing up until Saturday morning. Stevie was thrilled.

When Stevie got to her room, Terra was doing her nails with a layer of glitter over dark metallic, and then attaching faux diamonds. Stevie polished her own nails, following Terra's lead. She wanted to ask her about Kyle but wasn't sure how to broach the subject. Keeping her eyes on her fingernails, she groped for the right words. "Are ... have you ever been interested in Kyle?"

Terra laughed. "Been there, done that."

"What happened?" Stevie asked.

Terra was matter of fact. "It got boring."

Stevie tried to imagine how anyone could

ever get bored with Kyle. She wished she had the nerve to tell Terra about her crush. She just wasn't ready.

"Hey, what's the difference between a boy and a government bond?" Terra asked.

Stevie gave a blank look.

"Bonds mature," Terra replied.

Together, they giggled and pored over a particularly seductive magazine layout. The more they laughed, the more Stevie felt the urge to cough. Finally her cough erupted and she was unable to hold it in. She thought about using her Flutter to clear out her lungs, but decided against it. After several minutes, Terra looked concerned. "What's up with that? I've heard that cough before."

Stevie shrugged her shoulders and changed the subject.

Chapter 13

Saturday's class offerings were Caribbean dance, ballet, modern, improv, hip-hop, ballroom, jazz and African. Stevie was able to attend four during the day. She picked Caribbean and African in the morning. They were inspiring, but all the different styles made Stevie's head spin. In the afternoon she went to modern and ballroom. They were more relaxing than the tough morning workshops. All of the classes were dismissed by 5:00 so everyone could clean up and relax.

Back in the room, Stevie took a bubble bath and applied a mixture of body lotion and body shimmer she'd found in the hotel's gift shop. She'd read about this technique in a magazine and was thrilled to see that the combination worked: her skin glowed with a subtle shine.

Afterwards, she changed into a short red plaid dress with spaghetti straps and a long red trench coat. On her feet she laced up red Skecher combat boots. She decided to go frosty with her makeup, with icy-cool silver eye shadow and matching silver mascara. When her face had just the right amount of color, she slicked her hair back into a chignon and pushed two chopsticks through to keep it in place. Heather lent her a sparkly red tiara, and told her that she looked much older with makeup. Stevie was grateful for the compliment.

Dinner was at 7:00 at a nearby Mexican restaurant called Nachitos. By the time Stevie and Heather arrived at 7:15, the tables were overflowing with platters of turkey tacos, beef burritos, nachos with cheese, and chicken quesadillas. Baskets of chips were nestled between bowls of guacamole. Most of the dancers were drinking virgin margaritas.

"It's time to pig out with pleasure," Josh said, holding up a Shirley Temple. "Mia wants us to pay attention to the color foods ... is this red enough for you?

Stevie took one look at the drinks and high-fat foods on the table and knew she'd have to take more enzymes than usual. She glanced around the restaurant to find the ladies' room so she could sneak away without anyone noticing. It was towards the left, by Terra, who appeared to have streaked her light brown hair with tones of gold. Stevie sat down. She was dying to know how Terra had achieved this look, but didn't want to come across like a groupie, especially with Kyle sitting across the table. He was wearing a white crew-neck T-shirt under a black v-neck sweater with the sleeves pushed up over his elbows. His hair, wet from a shower, wasn't tied back in its usual ponytail, but hung on his shoulders. He looked like a model from a Calvin Klein ad.

Stevie marveled at Laura's ability to chat it up with him about their hip-hop class. Stevie felt herself about to stammer every time she opened her mouth. He was just so cute. Juliana and Fiona were laughing about a scene in a video. Bryan and Hale devoured tacos and enchiladas while Berge flirted with a waitress twice his age.

Eventually, Stevie ate a turkey taco, washing it down with a vanilla shake. The conversation moved from movies to music to makeup. Terra finally spilled about her tresses, explaining she'd used a comb-on hair mascara for the temporary shot of gold highlights. She said it worked just like regular mascara.

While the girls were listening to Terra, Stevie slipped away from the table to take her enzymes. Walking back, she grabbed a flyby plate of nachos and offered some to Terra, who brushed them aside and sipped a cup of something hot. Stevie noticed that she pushed the food around on her plate and rambled on. The torn tea wrapper by her cup was from a diet herbal tea. This wasn't healthy, Stevie knew. The nutritionist at the CF clinic had warned her that diet teas contained laxatives, which can cause diarrhea and dehydration. Stevie wondered if Terra had even eaten any of her food.

After dinner, everyone walked back to the convention center and reconvened in the lobby. Some members of Company decided to go to a revival theater nearby to see the 10:00 showing of *Saturday Night Fever*. Others wanted to check out the salsa band playing in the hotel's basement. Stevie opted for salsa dancing because that was where Kyle was headed. Mia said goodnight to everyone and reminded them that bed check was at midnight.

In the basement, Terra grabbed Kyle to dance. Stevie watched with envy as they made their way across the floor. An older boy Stevie didn't know asked her if she wanted to dance but she politely turned him down.

"Why not, munchkin?" he asked.

Stevie bristled. She hated any reference to her size. She tried to get away from him but he put his arms out to block her. She felt trapped, unsure of what to do.

Kyle looked over and saw Stevie could use some help. "Terra, Josh looks a little lonely. Go make his night," he said and then danced over to Stevie. Wordless, he flashed a grin, scooped her up, and twirled her around. The music was fast and rhythmic, and Stevie allowed herself to be swallowed up in it. After a time, the music slowed down, creating a completely different mood. Kyle dipped and turned her, then leaned back, pulling her with him. This was the first time Stevie had ever danced socially with a boy. She felt excited and nervous at the same time. She didn't really understand her feelings.

They danced and danced, stopping only to drink some water. When they finally quit for good, Stevie was astonished to realize that it was almost midnight. Kyle leaned down and held her face tenderly in his hands, then kissed her lightly on the lips. "Not bad dancing for a freshman," he said.

Walking back to her room, Stevie closed her eyes and smiled to herself. Giddy with excitement, she felt she couldn't possibly sleep, and she couldn't wait to see what would happen at after hours. She hadn't ever been away from home for the weekend. Even sleepovers were rare. Her mother limited them to once a month because she knew Stevie never got enough sleep. Those precious evenings out didn't begin until after treatment on Friday night and always ended with a pick-up Saturday morning so she could fit in her CPT. The idea of an after hours was beyond conceivable.

"What are you smiling about?" Josh asked as he breezed by her in the hallway.

Stevie felt herself blushing but said she was

thinking of a joke she'd heard earlier in the day.

"Thought maybe you were thinking about dancing with Kyle. I saw the way you looked at him," Josh teased.

Stevie was mortified. "He's a friend. I was just happy to be dancing," she said, as convincingly as she could.

"Yeah, right," Josh called after her.

Stevie opened the door to her room and saw that she'd gotten back before any of her room-mates. She thought about getting out her Flutter and going to the bathroom in the lobby to do a treatment before they returned. But not wanting to miss even a minute of the late-night fun, she decided against it. She rationalized that she'd had a lot of exercise that day, so skipping one more treatment wouldn't hurt. She fell on the bed, turned on the TV and waited for the others. When Heather, Laura and Juliana arrived a few minutes later, Laura told Stevie to get ready for bed. "If Mia even thinks you're going out, she'll send you home."

The girls took off their clothes, changed into pajamas, washed up and turned down their beds. At 12:07, there was a knock on the door and a voice boomed, "Bed check."

Heather opened the door to Mia, who marked on her clipboard as she called each girl's name. "Good night," she said, with a brisk smile. "Sleep well. We've got a busy day tomorrow."

As soon as she left, Laura jumped up from

her bed. "Give her ten and then we're outta here."

Stevie asked where they were going and what to wear.

"The pool in the back," Laura said. "And wear your pajamas. Easier to explain if we're busted."

Juliana announced that it was time to draw straws and told Stevie that someone had to stay behind in case Mia or a parent called.

"What do you say if they do call?" Stevie asked.

"Any excuse you can think of," Juliana answered.

"'She's in the bathroom' works," said Heather. "There's also, 'She went down the hall to get some ice.'"

"I like to say, 'She's in a really deep sleep. Do you want me to wake her?' They always say no to that," said Laura.

Juliana offered up the straws. "It's show time," she said, and motioned them over.

Stevie pulled one out, and then Heather got the short one. "Darn," she said. "I wanted to see that cute guy from Belmont High. You guys keep away. I'll have to wait until tomorrow to catch up with him."

Down by the pool, a group of 20 student dancers had parked themselves on a circle of chaise lounges and were gabbing about the revival of swing dancing. Someone had placed a cluster of votive candles in the middle near some incense. The scent was thick and cloyingly sweet. One of the girls from a different school claimed that swing had started up again at a club in San Francisco in 1989. A guy named Sawyer from a Pasadena arts school insisted that the movie *Swingers* had put Swing dancing back on the map. Stevie recognized him as the one Terra had picked out at the salsa bar in the basement. She watched Terra bat her eyelashes at him as she said that the Gap-khaki ad was another sign of swing-mania.

"Yeah," he said excitedly, "that's Louis Prima's original 'Jump, Jive an' Wail.'"

Stevie smiled to herself. He was hooked.

"It don't mean a thing if you don't dress for swing," Kyle rapped in a sing-song voice.

Stevie shivered in the cool air, and wrapped her arms around herself. Kyle was quietly crooning as the others kept on talking. She watched him, hoping he couldn't hear her heart pounding. Gradually, her pulse settled, and she just enjoyed his proximity.

"What's your snagging style?" Nellie asked, startling Stevie.

Stevie had no idea what she meant.

"How do you go after a guy," Nellie persisted.

"I don't know. I've never tried to snag anyone."

"I like to keep 'em guessing. Let a guy wonder how he can crack my code."

Stevie was mortified. Luckily, Jillian hunkered

down into a chair next to Nellie and distracted her. Stevie didn't want to admit she had a crush on Kyle and certainly didn't want to talk about it with Nellie.

By 2:30, the group had dwindled, leaving Stevie alone with Terra and Kyle. Stevie's cough started up but she did her best to stifle it. She watched Terra, who had sat down and snuggled close to Kyle. Even though Stevie knew they were just friends, she didn't like it. Almost as if Kyle was reading her mind, he gently moved away from Terra and got up. Then he reached into his pocket, pulled out a cigarette, and looked directly at Stevie, "Is there a reason I shouldn't smoke this in front of you?"

"Lung cancer, emphysema, heart disease," Stevie said. "Take your pick."

Kyle didn't let up. "Those are my choices 24/7. I want to know what it is about you."

The silence was deafening. Stevie wondered how long she could go without coughing.

"Is there a problem if I smoke in front of you?" Kyle persisted.

Stevie didn't answer, but Kyle continued to look her right in the eye. Clearly, he wasn't going to let her off the hook.

Eventually Stevie let out a deep, wet cough. She had a lot of mucus built up. Nodding, she felt defeated. "Second-hand smoke is very bad for me."

"That's a no-brainer," Terra said rolling her

eyes. "Everybody knows second-hand smoke can kill you."

Kyle looked indignant. "The people I'm around don't seem to be dying."

Pointing to his cigarette, she said, "I'm not going to die from that cigarette you're holding, either. But it really will hurt my lungs."

"Cut to the chase," Kyle demanded.

Stevie knew the moment had come for her to reveal what she had kept secret for so long. She took a deep breath and plunged ahead. "Have you ever heard of cystic fibrosis?"

Kyle thought about it for a minute. "I think so. Isn't there a football player with a kid who's got it?"

"Boomer Esiason. But his child is much younger than I am."

Terra looked bewildered. "What is it?"

Stevie tried to sound matter of fact. She wanted to keep her feelings in check. "It's a serious disease I was born with."

She could hear Kyle sucking in his breath. The sound broke the silence.

"It's not anything you can catch," she said quickly.

"Are ... are you going to die from it?" Terra asked

"We're all going to die," Stevie said, hoping to leave it at that. But when she gleaned from Terra's expression the fear in her face she knew she had to elaborate. "I think I'll be okay. Once in a while I might have to stay in the hospital."

"How did you get it?"

"I got one CF gene from my mom and another from my dad," she said. "If you only get one of the genes, you're a carrier with no symptoms. If you get two, you have CF."

"What are the symptoms?" Kyle asked.

Stevie said that CF gradually destroyed lung tissue and affected many of the body's other organ systems. "That's why I take so many pills," she added. "They're digestive enzymes and I need them to help me absorb food."

Frowning, Kyle quietly put his cigarette back in his shirt pocket.

There was an awful silence. Stevie wanted to ease the tension. "I'm hungry. Do you guys want to get something to eat?"

"I'll take a rain-check. It's past my bedtime," Kyle said as he grabbed his sweatshirt and headed off to bed. "See you guys at breakfast."

Terra leaned over and gave Stevie a hug. "I'm glad you shared that with us."

"I don't think Kyle is," Stevie said sadly.

Terra pulled back and put her arm on Stevie's shoulder, guiding her towards the hotel lobby. "It's a lot to digest. Let him chew on it overnight."

Chapter 14

The next morning, Stevie looked for Kyle but she couldn't find him anywhere. She was almost relieved. Staying up late and skipping treatment all weekend had left her looking terrible. And she didn't feel any better than she looked. Her lungs were filled with fluid, and she had no energy for dancing. She opted to skip morning classes and sat out by the pool instead. She thought about using her Flutter but it seemed easier to just lie low.

At least a dozen others had the same idea. Terra showed up around 11:00 looking like she had just rolled out of bed. Stevie asked if she had seen Kyle. Terra shook her head no. Nellie said Kyle had hitched a ride back to Riverdale with Josh.

Flipping through a magazine, she wondered

whether he would have left early just to avoid her. Unlikely, she thought, since she knew she wasn't that important to him. Still, he was gone, and Stevie wished she didn't have to wait until Monday to gauge his reaction to her disclosure.

Back at home on Sunday night, it was well after midnight when Stevie crawled into bed. She had stayed up late to finish the homework she'd neglected all weekend. Her lungs felt heavy, which made sleep difficult. She propped herself up with pillows, but still she tossed and turned, coughing intermittently. It crossed her mind that she hadn't called Clara once during the weekend. Stevie knew Clara would be upset.

Stevie started to drift off, but her cough flared up. Her mom staggered into Stevie's bedroom, half asleep. "You don't sound very good," her mother said, bleary-eyed. "I'm calling Dr. Bowman in the morning."

"I'm fine," Stevie protested.

"Want me to do CPT?"

"It couldn't hurt."

Stevie's mom went to get the paddles. When she came back, Stevie lay across her lap.

"So how was your weekend?" her mom asked, sounding more awake now. "I'd like to hear more about it."

Stevie had only told her mom that there had been lots of dancing and very big meals. "What do you want to know?" she asked, her voice warbling from the pounding.

"Did your dancing improve?"

Stevie was glad she was face down so her mom couldn't see her rolling her eyes. She didn't even know what questions to ask. "Mom, you're clueless. It wasn't about that."

"So, enlighten me."

"The weekend was about bonding with other members of Company. We need to feel like we're all on the same team."

"Did it work?"

Stevie lied. "Yep." She didn't want to tell her about Kyle's reaction to hearing she had CF. Hopefully, Stevie would see him in the morning and everything would be fine.

Stevie's cough had been an all-nighter, which definitely meant a clinic sentence. Her mom had called early and gotten Dr. Bowman to squeeze Stevie in. She dragged her daughter to clinic before school.

Jenna was the first member of the CF team to see Stevie. She observed the usual protocol of weighing and measuring her, and then administered the pulse oximeter test. Today she was way below her baseline of 95%, hovering around 89%. Not a good sign, Stevie thought.

Jimmy was the next one to come in and see her. Giving her the once over, he asked a few perfunctory questions and then commented on how raspy her voice was. "You been taking care of yourself?

Stevie averted her eyes. "Yes," she said, and wondered whether he would believe her.

"How often are you doing your airway clearance?"

"Same as always. Three times a day."

Jimmy took notes while they talked. "Are you doing chest percussion therapy or using the Flutter?"

"CPT at home — Flutter at school."

Stevie felt terrible about lying to Jimmy. He'd been her respiratory therapist since she was born and she was certain he could see right through her. But he didn't challenge anything she said. He told her to keep up the good work and said he'd see her later.

Nobody came in for a few minutes and Stevie could hear Jimmy talking to a patient in the hallway. "The most important thing about airway clearance is to do it. Try each of the choices and see which works best for you."

Just then the nutritionist came in. Cindy expressed concern that Stevie had lost five pounds since her last visit. Cindy asked if anything about her routine had changed, and if she was taking the time to sit down for meals. She asked what Stevie was eating for breakfast, lunch and dinner, and whether she was having any snacks. Stevie insisted she was taking her Ultrase and following her protocol, but she couldn't explain the loss.

Her mother speculated that dance company

was taking too much out of her. Stevie denied it, but her mom argued that Stevie had been away for a long weekend and had come back really run down. Stevie refused to acknowledge any connection between dancing and her decline. Cindy recommended that Stevie drink a Scandishake between meals. "It's a special drink loaded with 600 calories. It's an easy way to boost your overall intake."

"How does it taste?" Stevie asked.

"Hard to describe but I like it," Cindy said. She glanced at her watch. Lissa will be right in."

Right on cue, Lissa opened the door and gave Stevie a big hug. "You're a bag of bones, young lady. What do you think the doctor will say when he hears your lung function and weight are down?"

Stevie tried to sound convincing. "He'll tell me I need a new prescription and to come back in two or three months."

"I think he'll tell you that if you can gain weight on your own, he'll let you give it a try and have you come back in a month," Lissa ventured. "But he'll probably also say that if you can't do this, you can check in today and get a quick fix."

"I can't do the hospital at all," Stevie protested. "Concert is next month, and I have daily rehearsals."

Lissa wanted to know if Stevie was enjoying the dance company.

"Oh, yes," Stevie said.

Teasingly, Lissa asked if she was any good.

"Come see for yourself," Stevie challenged.

"I'd like to." Lissa said. " But we've got to reverse the weight loss, or you won't be strong enough to perform,"

Stevie hoped she wasn't going to give her a lecture. To her surprise, Lissa's comments were benign.

"I'll let you talk to the doctor about your options," she said as she left.

Shortly after, Dr. Bowman popped his head in the door. "Cindy tells me you think you're eating a lot. What did you have for dinner last night?"

"Chicken wings, a peanut butter and jelly sandwich, and a plate of brownies."

"Plenty of calories but not the most nutritious choices," he said. "Are you having many stomach aches?"

"No."

"Been taking your Ultrase?"

"I try to."

"Trying isn't good enough," Dr. Bowman said. "Your PFTs and your weight loss are way down. I need you to level with me. Have you been doing your treatments and taking your meds?"

"Not always. I'm sick of all this," Stevie complained. "It's embarrassing to take so many pills. And treatments take up too much time."

Dr. Bowman looked serious. "You've got to start taking better care of yourself. The more weight you lose, the more pulmonary problems you'll have."

Her mom said that ever since Stevie had started dancing with Company, she was always in a rush; she didn't spend as much time at home as she used to and it was harder to squeeze in the treatments. "Her cough has definitely increased in the past few months."

Dr. Bowman slipped the stethoscope under her shirt and listened to her lungs. "Is the stuff you're coughing up thicker than usual?"

"Yeah," Stevie said.

"Breathe. Again. Again. Once more. Are you coughing up any blood?"

"One time. I thought it was because I lifted weights."

Dr. Bowman put his stethoscope away. "I'm concerned about your increased cough, but I'm more concerned about the weight loss. Kids who are on the edge nutritionally can melt away in front of us."

Stevie knew that since both her weight and her lung function had dropped, she would probably need a hospitalization. Dr. Bowman wanted to culture her and try three weeks on Cipro, a very strong antibiotic. If it didn't work, he would recommend she be hospitalized for a tune-up. Stevie pleaded for another option. She couldn't start a hospitalization in three weeks because that would leave only one week before cleaning weekend. Concert was two days after that. She told Dr. Bowman that she couldn't go in for at least six weeks.

Dr. Bowman was sympathetic. "The only way I can guarantee you'll be at your concert in three weeks is to check you in today for a tune-up. We'll start you on an IV antibiotic and schedule you for CPT four times a day."

Stevie was desperate. "I've got an algebra mid-term on Friday and an English paper due next week. I'll do it if you promise to get me out in a week."

"I wish I could make that promise, but we need ten to fourteen days.

"That's too long," she cried.

"We might be able to shorten your stay if you're doing well and you're willing to go home with an IV in your arm."

"No way. Everyone would find out."

Dr. Bowman told Stevie they would play it by ear. "You might change your mind." Stevie agreed to be admitted voluntarily, but said she needed one more day to get her things together.

"Fine, but you'll get out one day later."

Her mom intervened. "Sweetie, why don't you get started today. I'll be happy to take care of everything."

"I need all my homework. They're really strict in Company. If you don't keep your grades up, you can't dance."

Her mom was determined. "We won't let that happen. I'll speak to your teachers."

"And Mia?"

Her mom nodded. "What about any of your friends?"

Stevie thought about having her call Terra and Kyle but decided against it. "Just Clara."

Doctor Bowman spoke. "I want you in the gym every day on the bike or the treadmill. There's no reason you can't practice your dancing up there, or in your room if you prefer. The more exercise you get, the better."

Stevie's mom gave a forced smile. For the first time since they'd gotten to clinic, Stevie really looked at her mom. Stevie felt bad; she knew the hospitalization would be much harder on her mother than it would be on her.

Chapter 15

During her previous hospitalization, Stevie's mom had stopped by every day before and after work. Stevie knew it killed her mom that she couldn't stay with her around the clock. Her mom used up all her vacation time each year taking care of Stevie when she stayed home sick, and taking her to clinic. She prided herself on never missing one of her daughter's medical appointments.

Hospitalizations were another story. Stevie's mom could call in sick for a few of the days, but she would lose her job if she didn't show up at all. Stevie told her mom not to feel bad; she could worry just as effectively at work as she could at Stevie's bedside.

The fact of the matter was, Stevie was bummed about being in the hospital and about having CF. Sometimes she felt that if she really let herself go, she would sob for hours and hours. With all the doctors, nurses and technicians who were in and out all day, there wasn't the privacy for that. During her worst moments, Stevie allowed herself five minutes of crying. That helped her keep a lid on things. Lying in bed with her IV and her television remote, Stevie felt lonely, isolated and small.

Three doctors came to see Stevie every day. Dr. Bowman was the attending physician. His routine was to come in each morning before 8:00. Training under Dr. Bowman was Dr. Winston, a "fellow," who was working on her post-residency specialty training. While Stevie was in the hospital, Dr. Winston trailed along with Dr. Bowman each morning. Once Dr. Bowman finished his hospital rounds, he left to see his out-patients in clinic.

Residents, the lowest doctors on the totem pole, popped in once or twice during the day. Stevie noticed that their hierarchy was similar to Company's — an apprentice ranked the same as a resident. She wondered if all of life worked like this.

While they were in the hall one morning, Stevie heard the docs talking. She got out of bed to hear them more clearly. Dr. Bowman was prepping a new resident about her. He explained that most people with CF are hospitalized because they have an increased cough and more phlegm. "They might feel like they've been run over by a truck," he said. "We also hospitalize for stomach-aches, weight loss and difficulty with breathing. Perhaps their coughing is waking them up at night. When patients are very sick, the middle of the night episodes are more frequent."

Dr. Winston said that Stevie's chart indicated she had a bad cough and that her weight was way down.

"She's in for a tune-up," said Dr. Bowman. "Big event coming up at school that she doesn't want to miss. We're giving her broad spectrum antibiotics."

When the doctors talked this way about Stevie, she got really depressed. Turning her back on them, she climbed into bed. Seconds later, Dr. Bowman knocked and then entered, trailed by the team of doctors. He greeted her warmly and then put his stethoscope under her shirt. Stevie longed for privacy. She hated this part, when all these doctors were gawking at her.

"Still a little crackling in the lower left lobe," Dr. Bowman said. "But overall you look pretty good. Are you doing okay?"

"I'd feel better if I could get some uninterrupted sleep. The nurses come in every few hours."

"Sleep is restorative, so we'll try cutting out middle of the night checks and see how you do," he said, and left, followed by his entourage.

Stevie looked forward to a good night's

sleep. Still, the prospect of another long day alone in the hospital filled her with *ennui*. Again, she could hear the doctors talking in the hall. She slipped into her bathrobe and followed them. Standing behind an open door, she listened as they conferred outside the next patient's room. She heard one of the residents ask Dr. Bowman if it was hard to deal with sick kids day in and day out. She smiled when she heard Dr. Bowman's response.

"It's terrible that any child has a disease like this. But Stevie's got a great mom. And she's still able to dance. There are lots of healthy kids out there from dysfunctional families who have it worse."

Shortly afterwards, Jenna came in. She had talked with Dr. Bowman and the nursing staff to see how Stevie was doing. Although Dr. Bowman gave the medical orders, it was Jenna who made sure everything happened like clockwork. For Stevie's hospitalization, that meant CPT four times a day, an IV line into her hand with two antibiotics, and three meals and three snacks daily. She popped her head into Stevie's room and asked how she was feeling.

"Not great. I don't want to be here," Stevie said. "And I hate this IV." She knew the needle stuck into her hand was the best way to get the drugs into her system. But being hooked up to a bag on a stand was really a drag.

Jenna's weary smile indicated she'd heard

this complaint before. "I know you'd much rather be at school with all your friends. In a matter of days you'll be back to your old routine."

Stevie wondered if that was what she said to all restless patients. She asked Jenna if there were other teenagers with CF in the hospital.

Jenna said there was another girl with CF down the hall, but Stevie couldn't spend any time with her because of cross-infection. "CF is not contagious, but CF patients are susceptible to chronic infection by bacteria resistant to antibiotics. Because of their susceptibility to these strains, hospitals generally keep CF patients away from each other."

"Why don't you invite some of your friends to come by?"

Stevie was wistful. "I don't really want anyone to know I'm here."

Chapter 16

When Clara showed up the next day, Stevie wondered if Jenna had asked her to come. It was a little too perfect to be a coincidence. Clara handed Stevie a gift-wrapped box from Paradise Thrift. Inside was a knee-length, black and white woolly dress with a boat neck.

"The sales girl said heavier fabrics are supposed to make you look bigger," Clara said. "The length and shape will also help."

Stevie, touched at her thoughtfulness, saw more tissue paper. Clara had also bought her a pair of white textured stockings. These were better for her than the dark opaque tights that were so popular at school, because they made her appear taller. Stevie felt her spirits lifting. She invited Clara to stay for a snack. "Tell me everything I've missed at school," she said.

Clara had plenty to tell her about Nellie's new boyfriend. "He's 19, and he rides a motorcycle!"

As they polished off a box of Oreos that Stevie had saved for just such an occasion, Stevie told Clara that Kyle didn't seem to know how to handle her having CF. "He took off right after I told him and I haven't seen or heard from him since," she said.

Clara was indignant. "He's the loser if he blows you off."

"It's not like we were an item," Stevie admitted. "I just had a huge crush on him."

A woman named Mrs. Rose arrived, carrying a large cup of coffee and a bag of cookies and cream malted milk balls. She had been sent by Child Life Services to spend an hour or two each day to help Stevie keep up with her schoolwork. Stevie was quite compliant, because she lived in fear of being kicked out of Company for falling behind in school. She hated doing the work, but at least Mrs. Rose provided a regular connection with school and the outside world. Besides, she was super nice.

"We'd better get started. You've got twice as much homework as usual," Mrs. Rose apologized.

"You've always said you don't want anyone's pity," Clara muttered. "I'd milk it for all it's worth and ask them to lighten your load."

"Dance concert is coming up. I've got to keep up, or they'll put me on academic probation."

Stevie was eating some dried apricots when

Dr. Bowman knocked and entered. "How's my favorite dancer?" he asked.

Dr. Bowman never dropped by mid-morning. Stevie tensed up, waiting to hear what had brought him to see her. Speaking in a slow, deliberate voice, he said that her culture wasn't clean. "You've been colonized by a bacteria called *Pseudomonas aeruginosa*. Your mother already knows, and asked me to discuss it with you."

Stevie was scared. She couldn't even pronounce the name. She licked her lips and tried to keep her voice steady. "Sounds serious."

"It might be. It's certainly a change. That's why we need to do an aggressive antibiotic treatment now. It's difficult to eradicate but we'll try. Your mother is coming by on her lunch break so we can talk about treatment."

"Is she worried? Am I contagious?" Stevie asked.

Dr. Bowman squeezed her shoulder and smiled. "Of course she's worried. But you're not a risk to other people."

Stevie grew teary. Bad news was part of living with CF, but Stevie still had trouble accepting a setback. Dr. Bowman recommended Cipro in pill form twice a day, and Tobi, an inhalable form of tobramycin, taken through a nebulizer. "*Pseudomonas* can be a recurring problem if we don't attack it properly."

Stevie used a tissue to wipe away her tears.

She sniffled. Dr. Bowman reminded her to blow her nose and cough as often as possible to bring the mucus up from her lungs. "Are you eating a lot and dancing regularly?" he asked.

Stevie scrunched her face up. "The food's inedible."

"Why don't you ask your mom to bring in some of those casseroles you like," Dr. Bowman suggested. His tone was encouraging. "I'm sorry you're stuck in here. I know we're messing up your plans a bit but we really want you to get well so you can dance in your concert." He picked up a dance magazine from Stevie's nightstand and smiled. "I'm waiting for the day I see you on the cover."

Around dinnertime, Cindy walked in carrying a large cup. "Brought you a Scandishake."

Stevie took it from her and drank about half of it. When she came up for air, Cindy asked what Stevie had eaten during the day.

"I wasn't hungry for breakfast, so I had an orange and half a bagel. Lunch was gross, so I asked the nurse to get me a hot dog and a bag of chips from the cafeteria."

"Did you drink anything?"

"Diet Coke."

"If you want to get out of here, you're going to have to eat more food. And you should drink regular soda, not diet. Is there anything I can get for you that would be more appealing than hospital food?"

"I love ice cream," Stevie said.

"You don't need me for that. Next time you get a soda, ask them to bring you a scoop of ice cream from the cafeteria and you'll increase your intake by a couple hundred calories. You will also be getting some much-needed fat."

Stevie grimaced. "If I add more fat to my diet, you'll make me take more enzyme pills."

"Not necessarily. We can give you higher dose capsules which will mean fewer pills, if you'd like. There are no restrictions on what you eat, but we do want you to have a well-balanced diet."

"How about bringing me a double cheese-burger and some fries?" Stevie said, grinning.

Chapter 17

It was raining the day Kyle and Terra came to visit. Stevie was sitting up in bed with her back to the door watching a rerun of *Dawson's Creek* and munching on buttered popcorn. She heard a knock on the door, but didn't think anything of it. Assuming it was one of her nurses, she didn't turn around but called out that it was okay to enter.

The sound of Terra's voice saying hello came as a surprise, and cheered her immediately. She turned and felt a sense of panic when she saw that Kyle was with her. Instinctively, her hand went to her head. Was her hair a mess?

"Brought you something to read," Kyle said. He handed her a beautiful hard-bound copy of *All God's Children Need Traveling Shoes*, by Maya Angelou.

Stevie was flustered. She couldn't believe he had remembered her favorite author.

"I'm sorry I was such a jerk in Palm Springs," Kyle said, sheepishly. "I just didn't know what to say."

"It's okay," Stevie said. Suddenly she realized she was wearing a hideous hospital gown. She quickly pulled the covers up so he wouldn't notice. Stevie wanted to reach out to him, hold his hand, but she knew he couldn't possibly feel the same way — her hair was ratty, her arm confined by the IV, and she hadn't showered since yesterday.

Terra brought her back to reality. "I still feel rotten about ruining your first secret buddy experience. This is your second gift," she said, holding up a leather bound blank book. "I have one, too," she said, holding it up. "I started writing in it a few weeks ago. It's been very cathartic. I thought it might help make the time pass more quickly."

"It couldn't hurt," Stevie said. "Although there's not much going on in here to write home about. Do you guys want the nurse to bring you some sodas?"

Both Terra and Kyle said yes, and Stevie buzzed for the nurse. She flipped off the TV and asked Terra what she'd been writing about.

Terra was evasive. "Nothing earth-shattering. Everyday stuff. The point is to let your feelings out."

"That's cool," Stevie said, then offered up

some of the chocolate candy her mother had brought in the day before. Terra declined, so Kyle, grinning, took two pieces. "One for me and ... one for me," he said. Then he changed the subject. "How are they treating you in here?"

Stevie shrugged. "Okay, I guess."

A good-looking resident popped in carrying sodas he'd gotten from the nurse. He asked how Stevie was feeling, but seeing her friends, he said he'd come back later.

"Could be worse," Terra said, watching the door. "You don't have to clean your room or help your mom make dinner. Nobody tells you what time you have to go to bed. You ask for a drink, they bring it immediately. Cute young doctors pop in and out."

They all laughed, but then Stevie got serious. "It's hard to explain," she began, "but I feel violated every time a doctor walks in the door."

Terra looked surprised. Kyle stared at her intently.

"The doctors do take care of you," Stevie continued. But they read everything about you in your chart before they come to see you. You feel like you're in a fishtank. There's a lot of personal info in your file that you might not want shared."

"I never thought about it like that," Kyle said.

Once she'd begun, Stevie couldn't contain herself. It was a relief to get it out. "There's no sense of your own space. People come in and out all day long. They physically invade you ... poke you with a needle for your blood and mess with your IV. And there's always a therapist coming in to do a breathing treatment or CPT. All they want to talk about is meal plans, medications and airway clearance techniques."

A nurse walked in to check Stevie's IV. No one said anything as she administered the IV meds.

"This is where journaling would really help," Terra said gently.

The nurse bent down to move a cord out of the way and noticed the pack of cigarettes in Kyle's shirt pocket. "I hope you know it's against hospital policy to smoke anywhere in the building."

Kyle nodded. After she left, he turned to Stevie. "I know I can't smoke around you."

Terra jumped in. "A lot of us just wish you'd quit."

"I know," he replied. Kyle walked to the window and looked down. "Are you going to be out in time for concert?"

"Yes," she said. "That's why I checked into The Riverdale Motel. I wanted to get it over with way before concert," Stevie said. Terra and Kyle chuckled.

"Will you be able to dance by then?" Kyle wanted to know.

Stevie straightened up in her bed. "Absolutely. I practice every day I'm here."

Terra glanced at the wall clock. It was 4:00. She gave Stevie a hug and said they should go.

"We're only a phone call away," Kyle said, leaning over to kiss her on the cheek. "At the very least, I want to know if you like the book."

"I'm going to start it tonight," she said. "Thanks for coming." Stevie was wistful. It was hard to watch them walk out the door.

Reaching over to her nightstand for the Maya Angelou book, Stevie spied two journals; Terra had left hers behind by accident. Stevie got out of bed and walked into the hallway. No sign of them. Stevie made a mental note to call Terra at her home in about half an hour.

Settling back into bed, Stevie opened Terra's journal. She knew she shouldn't read it, but she couldn't help herself. She determined that she would only take a peek but the first entry captivated her: "Mirror Fat." Stevie read the whole thing.

> *Look in the mirror. Fat.*
> *Thighs bulge and sway.*
> *Calves have flesh. It won't go away.*
> *Ribs are blanketed by a pale pudgy dough.*
> *It won't go.*
> *Breasts are useless but shrink they won't.*
> *They don't.*
> *Hips curve too much.*
> *They stay solid and stout.*
> *How did it come about?*
> *Well, I won't eat dinner.*
> *Just three bites. I'll be the winner. **Thinner**.*

Stevie was blown away. Had Terra really written these words? To Stevie, Terra was beautiful. She was strong and curvaceous; her movements had weight and her dancing was gloriously solid. Obviously, Terra didn't see herself that way. Did she wish to be scrawny like Stevie? At best, Stevie could be called "waiflike" or "delicate," and she knew that her dancing was ethereal only because she was light as a feather. Stevie would give anything to move with Terra's earthy power.

Page two didn't have a title.

> *They don't get it. They just don't.*
> *Maybe they can't. Maybe they won't.*
> *Why don't they understand,*
> *I'm alone in the dark?*
> *I live in a world, where only calories count,*
> *where food is as dangerous*
> *as a bloodthirsty shark,*
> *and the fears continue,*
> *they piece and mount.*
> *Just a carrot or an apple slice.*
> *Nothing more so I'll shrink.*
> *Sugar, spice, not so nice.*
> *Water is all that I'll drink.*
> *No messy food, nothing to eat.*
> *I CAN DO IT!*

Stevie set the book back down on her night-stand. She ached for her friend. Minutes later,

Terra came running back in. Her face was flushed. "I forgot my journal. Did you see it?"

Stevie pointed to the book and Terra grabbed it. Stevie felt like a voyeur. Should she tell Terra she'd read it? She could never admit that she'd opened Terra's journal without permission. Also, she didn't want to humiliate her.

A week passed and Stevie started to feel better. She buzzed the nurse to ask Dr. Bowman if she could go home soon. Dr. Bowman stopped by her room and said he'd need another pulmonary function test before he could release her. If things went well, he said, she could complete her therapy at home. Stevie went with her nurse to the PFT lab and did a series of tests that involved breathing into a machine. The mouthpiece that she was required to wear was uncomfortable. She breathed in and out, following the technician's instructions. A green TV monitor graphed out the results, showing how much air Stevie could take into her lungs.

The news was positive. Stevie scored 96%, well into the safe zone. She had also gained back three pounds. To keep it up, Dr. Bowman suggested she supplement each meal with a Scandishake and told her she could complete her antibiotic therapy at home. She promised Cindy that she would be good about taking her enzymes, and vowed to herself to be more diligent about her treatments.

Chapter 18

Gaining back three of the five pounds Stevie had lost was enough to get her out of the hospital, but all the attention to her weight had made her self-conscious about how small she was. For her return to school, Stevie decided to wear the dress from Clara. When she was ready, she looked in the mirror. "Trendy, not tacky," she told herself.

She couldn't wait to show Clara how she looked in her new outfit. She wanted to say so much more than "thank you." It struck Stevie how insensitive she'd been to Clara ever since she got into Company. But things were going to change.

En route to homeroom, she ran into Josh. He looked uncomfortable when he saw her.

"Welcome back."

"Is everything okay?" Stevie asked.

Josh was evasive. "Depends on who you ask. Have you seen anyone from Company?"

"Not yet. Only you ... why?"

Clearly uncomfortable, Josh told her that Mia had made some changes. Stevie asked him to be more specific.

Josh stammered. While he was hesitating, Kyle appeared and hugged Stevie. "We've missed you."

Stevie was thrilled. She momentarily forgot that Josh was trying to avoid delivering some unpleasant news. When Kyle pulled away, he ran his fingers across her cheek.

"You gave us quite a scare." Kyle said.

"I'm fine." Stevie said.

Josh looked quizzical. "So, what exactly was wrong with you, anyway?"

Kyle came to her rescue. "Stevie was just run down. It happens to the best of us. But we're going to keep an eye on her and make sure it doesn't happen again."

"That's probably why Mia made the change," Josh suggested.

"What change?" Stevie looked at both of them.

Again, Kyle hugged Stevie. "Mia put Megan in as Terra's understudy."

Stevie felt faint. Her eyes stung. She pressed her fingers to the inner corners of her eyes to keep from crying. How cruel of Mia to replace her, she thought. Why would she do such a thing? Stevie excused herself, saying she had to get to class. When she was out of sight, Stevie broke down, her tears flowing freely. Seeing other students walking in her direction, Stevie ducked into the bathroom to wash her face before her first class.

The day dragged on for Stevie. She wanted to confront Mia, to urge her to reconsider. When the final bell rang, Stevie grabbed her books and headed for the gym. When she got to the studio, Mia was working with Kyle and Megan. "Can we do it one more time, full out?"

Stevie watched in despair as Megan danced the steps that Stevie had practiced so many times. It wasn't fair, Stevie thought. Megan had her own piece and was dancing several other times. She didn't need to be Terra's understudy. Mia glanced at her watch and told Megan and Kyle to take a break. Kyle waved to Stevie and then left to get a drink. Megan grabbed a power bar from her backpack. Turning to Stevie, Mia flashed a welcoming smile and told her how good it was to have her back.

Stevie waited until Megan followed Kyle into the hall. When they were alone, she cornered Mia. "Why did you replace me?"

Mia was pleasant but firm. "I'm concerned about you. I don't want you to push yourself."

"I'm fine."

"It's not a rejection of you as a dancer," Mia said softly. "I'm just not sure you have the stamina for the extra rehearsal time it takes to understudy all of Terra's dances. Being in the hospital must have taken its toll on you.

"It was a tune-up," Stevie said. "A voluntary admission."

"You were gone for a long time. Concert is just around the corner. We had to keep going."

"I danced every day in the hospital gym. I know the material backwards and forwards," Stevie pleaded.

Mia didn't budge. "You're a freshman. You've got three more years."

"Terra is graduating. I'll never get to work with her again," Stevie cried.

"You'll still dance in the big group numbers," Mia explained. "I only replaced you as the understudy."

"But …"

Mia cut her off. "I'm afraid my decision is final. We can't afford to jeopardize your health."

Members of Company began trickling in. Stevie recognized defeat, but she was saddened by the finality of Mia's words. Terra came over to Stevie and embraced her. "It's great to see you here. You look wonderful."

Stevie wanted to return the compliment, but Terra looked terribly thin. Instead, she thanked her. "I'm so happy to be back," she added.

Mia announced that it was time to rehearse "It Don't Mean A Thing." "We're going to re-block the third section."

Stevie wanted to make one last-ditch effort to get Mia to change her mind. She knew Megan didn't give a hoot about being Terra's understudy. Mia's action seemed almost punitive. Stevie watched Mia carefully during rehearsal to see what kind of a mood she was in.

After everyone was dismissed, Mia headed back to her office. Stevie, giving her a few minutes to get settled, turned to Juliana to ask if she could copy her notes to study for their upcoming science test. "I promise to have them back to you first thing in the morning."

Juliana offered to photocopy them for her. "I'm sure you have a lot to catch up on."

Stevie remembered how worried she'd been that she would never fit in at Company. She felt lucky to have been chosen as an apprentice, but, even more, she was grateful to have been accepted. She thanked Juliana, said good-bye and headed for Mia's office. When she got there, the door was ajar, and she overheard Mia talking. "I'm concerned about Terra. She's lost a lot of weight."

Stevie realized Mia was talking to Mr. Burdulis, the volleyball coach, since they shared an office. But Stevie didn't hear anyone speaking. After a few minutes Mia said that dropping so much weight in such a short time might be an indication that Terra had a problem.

Stevie assumed that Mia was talking on the telephone to Terra's mom. Or, to be more accurate, listening to her, since Mia didn't say anything for what seemed like a very long time. Finally, Mia spoke, and she was grave. Her words sounded carefully chosen. "Terra may have an eating disorder. I think she should see a doctor."

Seconds later, Mia cried out loud. "She hung up on me!" This time Mr. Burdulis did answer. "You need to have a chat with the counselor." Backing away, Stevie knew this was not the best time to approach Mia. Stevie was worried about Terra and knew what she had to do.

Chapter 19

When it was time for Stevie's follow-up appointment, she asked her mom to schedule it for 10:00 a.m. so she wouldn't have to miss rehearsal. This time, the waiting room was packed. There was a girl who looked about the same age as Stevie, seated in the corner reading *Seventeen Magazine*. Her appearance frightened Stevie. She was pasty white, with dark circles under her eyes. Her cough seemed to shake the waiting room.

Deeply disturbed, Stevie wanted to ask her why she sounded so bad but she didn't know how to approach her. People just didn't talk to each other in the clinic waiting room. Finally, she got up from her chair and walked over to her. She felt all eyes on her as she introduced herself and asked the girl her name.

The girl looked startled. "Barbara."

"Is this your usual cough or are you having an episode?"

"I guess my disease is progressing. I've also been really bad about my treatments. Do you ever skip?"

"Sometimes," Stevie acknowledged. "But my mom hovers pretty hard."

"Mine did, too. But now I'm at college. It's hard being on your own."

Stevie was struck by the fact that this girl was old enough to be in college. She didn't look older than 15. Stevie felt an immediate sense of urgency about her treatments. She knew that even if a patient was 100% compliant, the disease would still progress. But skipping treatments definitely aggravated an already serious situation. Stevie sat down by her mother.

In the car driving home, Stevie thought about how lucky she was. Dr. Bowman said the protocol had been successful – her *Pseudonomas* was under control, and her lung function and weight were back up. She felt strong and ready for concert. It could be a lot worse.

Stevie got to the gym at 7:15 on the first morning of cleaning weekend. Terra stood at the far end of the hallway outside Studio A, sharing a laugh with Josh and Heather. Kyle was reading *Spin Magazine* when Stevie walked over to him. Her hair was styled in an angel's braid, with fine pieces of hair around her hairline braided down the center from front to back. The back was completely tucked under. Kyle let out a whistle when he saw her. Stevie blushed.

She tossed a celebrity magazine in his lap with the headline, "I Was Dying To Be Thin." He looked up, puzzled. Stevie didn't say a word. She looked back and forth between the magazine and Terra.

Kyle stood up and led Stevie away from Terra. "You think?"

Stevie began tentatively. "I was reading this article. It sounds like Terra."

"You think she's anorexic?" Kyle sounded truly surprised.

"I don't know, but she's gotten really thin lately. And when we went out for breakfast the other day, she didn't eat."

"Maybe she wasn't hungry. Sure you're not overreacting?"

"You tell me when you hear the rest."

"There's more?"

Stevie told him about the poems she'd read in Terra's journal and about what Mia had said. "Terra has a problem, and we need to talk to her about it," she finished.

"No way," he shook his head. "What could we possibly say to her?"

"That we're concerned. That we're here if she wants to talk. If she doesn't, we'll let it go."

Kyle wanted to think about it. He said he

wasn't sure how they should approach Terra. Stevie suggested they invite her to get an ice cream with them after school. Kyle didn't think it was appropriate to do it around food.

"You're right. Do you have a better thought?"

"I wish I did," Kyle said, sighing.

Stevie brightened. "How about if you offer to drive her home and we talk about it in the car."

Kyle agreed.

After school Stevie rushed to the parking lot and climbed into Kyle's back seat. She let Terra get in front with him. Terra flipped on the stereo. "Thanks for the ride," she said. "I'm exhausted."

"Is everything okay?" Kyle asked.

"Why wouldn't it be?" Terra sounded defensive. Stevie, who was watching the side of Terra's face for any reaction, thought she saw a flash of panic. It passed quickly, but Stevie was sure she had seen it.

"You've lost a lot of weight. You look very thin." Stevie asserted.

"Isn't that like the pot calling the kettle black?" Terra countered, defensively.

Kyle cut in. "Stevie's worried about you and so am I. Losing too much weight can be dangerous."

Terra leaned in to Kyle and pointed an accusatory finger at him. "How dare you. You smoke like a chimney."

Kyle was indignant. "I don't smoke that much."

Ignoring him, Terra turned to Stevie. "And

you!" she said with an edge in her tone. "You don't do your treatments. Don't talk to me about dangerous. Stop the car. I'm getting out."

"Please, don't," Kyle pleaded. "We're only trying to help."

"Pull over." Terra started to open the door.

Kyle looked in the rearview mirror at Stevie. She raised her shoulders to indicate she had no clue what to do. He drove to the corner and stopped. "We blew it!" he said after Terra had gotten out.

Stevie nodded in agreement.

Chapter 20

During rehearsal for "Black Widow," Terra was unable to stand steady. Mia noticed and asked her flatly, "When was the last time you ate?"

Terra looked offended. "I eat."

Pressing on, Mia asked, "What have you eaten today?"

"I had an apple." Terra said dismissively.

"When did you eat the apple?"

"Last night."

"What have you eaten today?" Mia repeated herself.

"I had a diet Coke."

"That doesn't count. I don't want to see your face until you've eaten a meal."

Terra burst out screaming. "Why is everyone so obsessed with my weight?"

What is she doing to herself, Stevie wondered. She went into her backpack and pulled out a bag of granola. She offered it to Terra, but her friend just sailed past, ignoring her.

When Terra showed up the next day, she looked pale. Mia asked her whether or not she had eaten breakfast. Terra said that she had had an egg white omelet and a piece of whole wheat toast. Judging by the look on Mia's face, Stevie could tell she didn't believe a word Terra said. Mia told everyone to get in position to dance "Black Widow."

Terra stretched her arms and turned in *arabesque*. Stevie watched as Terra, coming out of the turn, grew short of breath, causing her to halt. Terra stopped turning, but looked as if she thought the room hadn't. She stuck her arms out in an apparent attempt to regain her balance, but it didn't work. She twitched, then stumbled over her own feet before standing back up.

Stevie moved towards her, unsure what to do. By this time, Terra had started swaying and looked as if she were enveloped by vertigo. Kyle ran to her and offered his arm. He guided her towards the front of the auditorium, but after a few steps, she collapsed.

Mia rushed over and briskly tapped her cheeks to see if she was okay. She turned her head and yelled for Juliana to call 911. Everyone crowded around. Mia called out for a coat.

Heather handed one to Mia, and Mia covered Terra with it. In a calm but commanding voice, Mia sent everyone to the studio next door, and asked Kyle to run the rehearsal. She told Stevie to get a cold, wet towel for Terra's forehead.

Mia used the school phone to call the office. "Get a hold of Terra Reede's mother. She's passed out."

Within minutes, the vice principal came running in with a walkie-talkie. "We called her mom. Should she meet Terra at Riverdale Hospital or come here?"

"The hospital. I'm expecting the paramedics any minute," Mia said.

The vice principal got on the walkie-talkie and repeated what Mia had said. Terra's eyes fluttered open. Mia leaned over her and whispered, "Terra, you're okay. You passed out. Do you know where you are?"

Terra was very weak. "Rehearsal."

Mia breathed a sigh of relief. The paramedics arrived. They lifted Terra onto a gurney, popped it up and wheeled her out into the ambulance.

Stevie walked into the next room as Kyle was warming everyone up. He prepped them for "Black Widow," then told everyone to get in their opening positions. He called out for Megan to fill in for Terra, but she wasn't in the room.

Josh was the first to respond. "Megan hasn't been around for a few days."

"I thought she was the understudy," Kyle

said, perturbed.

Juliana cleared her throat. "She's been having problems in biology."

"So what?" Kyle demanded. "She should be here. Let's take it from the top. We'll work around her."

Kyle turned on the music and they ran through the dance.

Mia walked in and called for Stevie to dance with Kyle. Stevie was taken aback. "You said Megan was going to be the understudy."

"As of yesterday, she's on academic probation. She can't dance until next semester," Mia explained.

Stevie came forward tentatively. She knew the steps backwards and forwards, but that didn't stop her from feeling that she wouldn't be able to get through it. Mia sensed her apprehension and offered words of encouragement. "I've seen you do it. You're going to be fine. The only thing holding you back is your own fear."

Stevie took a deep breath. She asked if they could run some of the lift sequences first.

"Let's do it," Kyle said.

He lifted Stevie up above his head, then slowly brought her down. She dropped to the floor, slid around his legs and was propelled up by him again. Their movements were accurate and precise, and Stevie felt her confidence returning. She focused her mind on the counts, steps and patterns she had to follow. After that, it was easy to run the entire number. At the end, Mia gave Stevie a big hug and said how proud of her she was for saving the dance.

The next day, they were back for the full dress rehearsal in the auditorium. Stevie and Kyle were dancing "Black Widow" when Terra arrived. Mia was backstage, finalizing wardrobe assignments. Terra walked to the tape player and shut off the music. She apologized to everyone for missing rehearsal yesterday. Stevie winced when she saw how pale Terra was.

Terra extended an extra thank you to Stevie for filling in, but said she was back and ready to dance. Stevie, hiding her disappointment, quickly stepped aside. Terra moved into position, and called out for someone to cue up the music.

Mia walked in and put her hand up in the air to signal that Terra should stop dancing with Kyle. "Terra, you're out. You lost your chance."

"But I'm here," Terra exclaimed.

Kyle looked concerned. "Are you strong enough?"

"I'm better," Terra said calmly.

Mia looked doubtful. "You have a problem that can't be solved in a day. Especially the day before concert."

"Trust me, I'm fine."

"Look at you. You're still very weak. And I have a show to produce."

"That's ridiculous. I can do it. And you know

no one can dance this piece better than I can."

"You were warned."

"It's my last show. Don't take it away from me."

"I'm sorry. Stevie is dancing."

Fighting back tears, Terra walked out. Company members stood by silently, not knowing what to say or do. Mia recognized that she needed to rein in the group. "We're going to run 'Black Widow' from the top. Those of you not in the number, please take a seat in the audience. When we finish, we'll go straight into the finale."

Stevie and Kyle danced together in perfect unison. It was a bittersweet victory for Stevie, who knew Terra's heart was broken.

Chapter 21

That night at dinner, as she picked at her lasagna, Stevie tortured over Mia's inflexibility. Why wouldn't she let Terra dance? Was she really worried about her fainting, or was it more complicated?

Her mom frowned at Stevie. She could see that Stevie felt responsible. "It isn't your fault," she said.

"That's not the point. Terra is the one who should be dancing tomorrow, not me."

Her mother put down her fork. "Why don't you call Mia at home? See if she's had a change of heart."

"That's not a bad idea," Stevie agreed, as wheels began turning in her mind. She ran upstairs, looked up Mia's number in the school directory, and dialed. Stevie was relieved when

Mia answered. "Hi, it's Stevie. I'm worried about concert."

Mia expressed surprise. "But you were great."

"I'm feeling insecure about the piece. It was just luck I remembered all the steps. One more rehearsal before the performance would definitely help me."

"Tomorrow is opening night. I don't like anyone dancing the day of a show."

"Please. It would give me the confidence I need."

"If it's that important, you can do it a half hour before we open the house. Just make sure it's okay with Kyle and the others."

Stevie thanked Mia for being so understanding and hung up, grinning like the Cheshire cat. She dialed Terra's number and asked Mrs. Reede if she could speak to Terra. When Terra picked up, Stevie simply said, "We've got to talk. I'm on my way over."

Early the next evening, Stevie did an extra long treatment. She wanted her lungs as clear as possible for the concert. When she slipped into the back of the auditorium, an hour before show time, she saw Kyle was in full dress practicing his part, stage right. Periodically he glanced around to look for Stevie, but he didn't see her. He walked center-stage and called out to Mia, who was in the audience, third row center.

"Should I slow the second sequence down a little? It seemed rushed during yesterday's rehearsal."

"No. It looked great," Mia said.

With the lights shining right in his eyes, Kyle couldn't see much. Holding his hand over his forehead as a shield, he asked Mia if she knew where Stevie was. "She said she'd be here at 6:00."

Terra walked on stage wearing her costume. "I'm here instead," she said.

Mia stood up. "You were replaced."

Terra was resolute. "I'm not going to let you do this. At least let me show you I can still dance."

"No," Mia said, looking around. Stevie should have been here by now."

"She's not coming for another half hour," Terra stated.

Kyle and the other dancers looked surprised.

"She wants me to dance. She knows I deserve to. That's why she asked for one final rehearsal."

Realizing she had been set up, Mia was furious. "I'd cut the piece if it were only a solo. But that wouldn't be fair to Kyle."

"Give me a chance, please."

Mia shot her an angry look. She didn't like being backed into a corner. She called out to the crew to start up the music. From the P.A. system, the sweet strains of the music began, and Terra took her position. Kyle shrugged and moved to his side of the stage.

"Let's see it," Mia said.

Terra danced a strong run-through. Stevie saw that Mia was impressed. Still, at the conclusion, Mia expressed irritation. "I've been set up and I don't like it."

Stevie walked down the aisle from the back of the auditorium. The hardest part for her was knowing that her teacher was angry. Stevie willed herself to remain strong and not let Mia see right through her calm facade. "It really is Terra's dance. I'm fine with it."

Mia threw her arms into the air in resignation. "Looks like I'm outnumbered," she said.

Stevie sighed with relief, then gave Terra the "okay" sign with her fingers.

Mia looked harshly at Terra. "You owe Stevie a debt of gratitude for this. She earned the right to dance and she's stepping aside for you. I find that remarkable." Then she looked at her watch and said they should finish getting ready.

Stevie joined the rest of Company already downstairs in the Green Room, the crowded make-up area with wall-to-wall mirrors and vanity tables piled with cosmetics and hairpins. Adrenaline was running high among the dancers, who were flitting about, applying last-minute makeup touches and stretching their muscles.

Chapter 22

Company made their way up the stairs and took their opening places. The lights in the auditorium were dimmed, and a pre-recorded voice welcomed the audience, reminding them not to take photographs of any kind. The first number, with full cast on-stage, was called "Bring It On." It was upbeat, with a lot of jazzy movements and humor. Designed to engage the audience, it was a great opener. Stevie knew that the piece was working as they performed; then at the end, the applause went on for so long, the next dance had to be held for a few minutes.

Afterwards, Stevie watched from the wings until the finale. Standing in the shadows, she saw that whenever Terra was on-stage, all eyes were on her. Terra was a captivating performer. Several more dances followed, and then it was time for Terra's big number.

"Black Widow" was the best it had ever been. There was an electricity between Kyle and Terra, a hypnotic quality that drew the audience in. Even though Stevie had watched them do it over and over again, tonight it was somehow different. Terra threw her soul into the dance in a way she had never done before. It was as if she realized how lucky she was to be dancing at all.

The second to last piece was "Caffeine Jitters, Good Morning L.A." It was an abstract piece, modern in both movement and music. Choreographed by Laura, who had lived in L.A. before moving to Riverdale, the dance used geometric shapes to explore form, space and time. Its mood was frenetic, bringing to life the rushed pace of Los Angeles. The three dancers didn't look at each other; it was a portrayal of the indifference she felt permeated L.A.

The finale was a full Company swing number called "It Don't Mean A Thing." It was high intensity. Company dressed in vintage clothing, with Kyle in a zoot suit with a fedora, and black and white spectator flats. Terra wore a bright red dress that flared from the waist, bobby socks and Mary Jane shoes. They were partners again, center-stage, and their steps were fast and lively. Stevie and the other dancers surrounded them, and every now and then someone in the audience let loose a cheer or cat call.

When the lights went out and the dancers

stood panting in their final poses, it was as if the energy from the piece flowed to the audience. The room surged with emotion, and the crowd leapt to a standing ovation. The dancers took a bow, and the curtain went down. The curtain came back up, and Terra stepped forward and bowed again. A handsome young man walked to the stage and handed her two dozen long-stemmed red roses. Then the house lights came up, the curtain went down again, and the show was over.

In the first moments after the curtain fell, there was a collective feeling of shock; opening night was over. Backstage, the dancers kissed, hugged and congratulated each other, and began to take their costumes off. In one breath, Mia congratulated the cast, and in the next, she yelled out to hang up clothing properly and put away makeup.

Josh reminded everyone that the cast party was Saturday after the final show. At the party, everyone would reveal their secret buddies. Stevie looked forward to seeing Josh's face when he found out that she'd been his secret buddy.

Terra walked up looking radiant.

"You were fabulous," Stevie gushed, giving her a hug. "Your dancing was never better."

Kyle waited for the moment to pass, which happened when other cast members swarmed Terra. Then he turned to Stevie and asked what had happened with Terra. Stevie feigned ignorance.

"You had your shot to dance Terra's part and you let it go," Kyle pressed. "I want to know why."

Stevie was calm. "It was Terra's piece. I couldn't take it away from her."

Terra pulled herself away from the crowd and turned to Stevie. "I guess I should say thank you for that Scandishake." She paused and then added, "Not that I really needed it."

Kyle rolled his eyes. "I don't know what a Scandishake is but there must have been something special in it to get you back on your feet so quickly," he said.

Terra winked. "Stevie's always known how to put me in my place. I even promised to clean my plate from now on."

Terra's mother arrived with a bouquet of flowers. Kyle gave Stevie a loving punch. "You should feel really proud of yourself." Hearing a noise, he turned and saw that more people from the audience were filing in with flowers.

A couple that Stevie didn't know walked up to Kyle and congratulated him. "Great job," the guy said. "How about celebrating with a smoke outside?"

Kyle looked at Stevie. "Thanks for the offer but I'm taking a pass."

The girl shrugged and the two of them moved off.

Stevie looked at Kyle. "It's okay. You can go if you want."

"Didn't I tell you? I quit," Kyle said slyly.

"By the way, I'm ready for that rain-check now."

Stevie looked puzzled. Kyle grinned. "The dance convention, out by the pool. You asked if anyone wanted to grab a bite. If the invitation still stands, I say let's go get something to eat."

Stevie's face lit up. Kyle slid his arm into Stevie's and they sneaked out.

Under the stars, Stevie turned to face Kyle. "You were incredible tonight."

Kyle cut her short. "You're the incredible one. I still can't believe what you did for Terra."

"Not for Terra, but for Company. It was a better show with Terra dancing 'Black Widow,'" she said firmly, and meant it.

"Well, soon, it'll be your time."

"Maybe," she said. But standing beside him, having danced with Company, she knew it was her time already.

Acknowledgements

This book was made possible by a grant from Axcan Scandipharm Inc.

I would like to thank the following people for their help on this book:

- Dale Brakhage and Thom Rowland, for sharing my vision;
- Janet Roston, Artistic Director of the Advanced Dance Theater Group of Beverly Hills High School, and Company 1999, for illuminating the world of dance, step by step;
- Bill Taub, CF social worker extraordinaire at Duke University Medical Center, for his keen insight about issues affecting teenagers with CF;
- Dr. C. Michael Bowman, for devoting his vast knowledge of medicine to this project;
- Meryl Shader, for her creative input, her meticulous editing and her gift with words;
- Joyette Jagolino, for clarifying CF protocol;
- Laura Karlin, Company 1999, for helping me

return to teen life;

• Cambria Gordon, for revealing the structure of the young adult novel;

• Eric Lax, Karen Sulzberger, Abigail Jones, David MacFarland, Myra Lurie, Julie Robinson and Terra Pasternak, for their editoral comments;

• Duke University Cystic Fibrosis Center, for allowing me access to their patients and staff;

• Martha Donze for her proof reading;

• Suzette Allan, for serving as my liaison to Axcan Scandipharm;

• Jason Newman for letting me interview his high school students;

• Jay Jackson, for the exquisite cover art;

• Cindy Karlan Cohen, for her painstaking work in design and layout; and

• Dick Chandler and Media Lithographics, for their printing.

A special thank you to Mark, my love, who makes it all possible, and to Micah and Mallory who make it all worthwhile.

About the Author

Diane Shader Smith is the author of *Mallory's 65 Roses* and *A Dialogue With Cancer*. She spent five years on the writing staff of the ABC-TV series, *General Hospital*, and two years writing for KIIS Radio in Los Angeles. She has written extensively for newspapers and magazines, and has edited several books. Diane lives in Los Angeles with her husband and two children.

ADEK®, FLUTTER®, SCANDISHAKE® and ULTRASE® are trademarks owned by or under license to Scandipharm, Inc. ULTRASE® and ULTRASE® MT are manufactured by Eurand International, Milan, Italy, using its DIFFUCAPS® and EURAND MINITABS® technology for Scandipharm, Inc.

We would like to acknowledge Pathogenisis, maker of TOBI and Bayer, maker of Cipro for their continued efforts on behalf of children with cystic fibrosis.